"..........................ness?"
he asked disarmingly

Refusing to be taken in, she reminded him, "You said gauche."

"Well, yes, perhaps a little of that, no?" He raised black eyebrows. "Your lovely black leather makes you look sleek and sophisticated, Miss Mulgrove," he went on, "but underneath I suspect there remains the frightened, confused little girl I saw yesterday...sprawling so charmingly on the floor at my feet."

Tiffany gasped and when she leaned over to put her empty glass on the table, her hands were shaking.

Harlem Barensky laughed. "I think that rather proves my point."

"What proves your point?"

"You're so easily disconcerted." He seemed to move closer but it was only his voice that changed. "Keep cool, Miss Mulgrove. There will inevitably be worse to come."

SALLY HEYWOOD is a British author, born in Yorkshire. After leaving university, she had several jobs, including running an art gallery, a guest house and a boutique. She has written several plays for theater and television, in addition to her romance novels for Harlequin. Her special interests are sailing, reading, fashion, interior decorating and helping in a children's nursery.

Books by Sally Heywood

HARLEQUIN PRESENTS
1200—FANTASY LOVER
1235—TODAY, TOMORROW, AND FOREVER
1256—LAW OF LOVE

HARLEQUIN ROMANCE
2925—IMPOSSIBLE TO FORGET
3074—TRUST ME, MY LOVE

SALLY HEYWOOD

love's sweet harvest

Harlequin Books

TORONTO • NEW YORK • LONDON
AMSTERDAM • PARIS • SYDNEY • HAMBURG
STOCKHOLM • ATHENS • TOKYO • MILAN

Harlequin Presents first edition October 1990
ISBN 0-373-11306-4

Original hardcover edition published in 1990
by Mills & Boon Limited

CHAPTER ONE

THE second the taxi screeched to a halt Tiffany threw herself out and thrust a five-pound note into the outstretched hand of the driver. 'Keep the change,' she gasped, regretting the lentil soup that would be her staple diet for the rest of the week, then she hurled herself across the pavement into the art college entrance.

Just her luck to have had her twenty-first birthday celebrations the night before! She'd wanted to be in early today even if it was only because of a rumour . . .

When she had left the shared house in Tottenham just now she had left behind several unidentified mounds sleeping about the place. Fashion students, painters, a sculptor or two, she guessed, not bothering to peer too closely as she hurriedly put herself together, and none of them her own crowd. That in itself was ominous and gave the rumour credibility.

Patting wisps of dark curly hair back into the ribbon at her nape as she hurried two at a time up the stairs, she couldn't help smiling. It had been quite a party. And totally unexpected. Trust Ginny and Pat to surprise her like that! Last night she had been dog-tired when she got home, having worked on her exhibition project till nine. A party had been the last thing on her mind as she had gone into what she had imagined to be an empty house. All the lights had been out. Then, suddenly, the minute she had stepped in through the door a blaze of light had greeted her. 'Happy birthday, Tiff!'

'Surprise, surprise!' A grinning Pat had waved a bottle, and then the whole crowd had emerged from the next room.

Everybody had been there, even the landlord. That last had been Ginny's idea. Tactful to the last! In the circumstances Tiffany could hardly have said that all she wanted to do was sleep, and think of the next day.

Now she sped round the corner, puffing slightly as she reached the third floor. The theatre design people, her own crowd, had been conspicuous by their early departure well before dawn, and she guessed that, like her, they had all made a supreme effort to get in early this morning. Vaguely remembering Ginny's voice in her ear at some unearthly hour and how she had turned over for another ten minutes, she thrust her wrist out and snatched a quick glance at her watch. Heavens! Nearly twenty minutes late! Normally it wouldn't matter a damn and she would make it up later, but today was whispered to be special.

Rumour had spread like flame in a hayrick when a secretary from the principal's office had let fall a hint that a group from the National Ballet had asked for a tour of the theatre design studios. Talent spotting for some show? Nobody really knew, but it was enough to spread excitement like wildfire.

Later the rumour was confirmed when a discreet word passed from the head of department to the lecturers, and they in turn passed it on to the tutors and the final-year students, 'Be there. Be bright. You may catch somebody's eye.' That had been the gist of the message.

One or two students in her year had already landed jobs, one with a theatre company in the provinces, another with a television company in South London. Tiffany herself was after something like that. Ballet didn't appeal to her much. But a job was a job. And soon they would all be out on their ears, diplomas clutched in their sticky little hands, portfolios under their arms, and the prospect of endless trudging round the studios looking for prospective employers before them.

Now she skidded to a halt. The double doors leading into the high-arched studio were closed. Standing on tiptoe she could just see through the glass, and her gaze came slap up against the suited shoulders of some strangers. So she'd dished her chances already!

The principal's grey head came into view for a moment and, craning her neck, Tiffany spotted four or five visitors. Three, she corrected, as they disappeared behind a partition. Two men and a woman. The other two were staff. She waited until the group was safely out of sight, then took her chance. With the utmost caution she pressed open the double doors and slid inside. By edging along one side of the central aisle she could get to her place without being too obtrusive.

Rafe had the corner just inside the door, and his work had evidently already been give the once-over for he grinned when he saw her. 'Naughty, naughty!' he murmured, glancing ostentatiously at the clock on the wall. There was an unnatural silence from the rest of the class, hidden behind their drawing boards.

'Shut up, Rafe. Have they been up at our end yet?' Tiffany whispered back.

'They've just come in. Progress is slow because they're too busy having their boots licked by Willie Wonka.'

'Suits me!' She dazzled a smile of relief, and began to edge her way up the aisle behind the visitors.

Perhaps because she was too busy trying to catch a glimpse of them, and not looking where she was going as she swerved past

Rafe's work-bench, the flared sleeve of her wool coat snagged the corner of a tray of drawing inks. Before she could stop herself, she lunged forward to try to catch it, and somehow managed to trip, knocking over the entire table and its multicoloured contents, and sprawling full length among the whole lot.

'Hell!' she exclaimed loudly as she went down in a flurry of skirts and long hair.

There was an ominous silence. Rafe was standing like a statue, looking not at her and the mess she'd made, but beyond her to the other side of the room. From her position on the floor she slowly turned and looked up.

The entire party—principal, head of department, tutor, and the three visitors from the National Ballet Company—had reappeared from around a partition and were gazing down at her in astonishment. Her eyes flicked from the familiar faces of the staff, their expressions making varied studies in dismay, to seek out sympathy elsewhere. But the three strangers seemed equally appalled.

Of the three the woman was the only one to make a movement, and she brought one exquisitely well-groomed hand to a vivid red mouth that had formed itself into a perfect though silent O. Then her companion, a short fair man with a receding hairline, stepped forward. 'Quite an entrance.' He held out a hand to help her up. But her own gaze was now riveted by the man standing directly behind him.

He appeared to have dissociated himself entirely from what was going on. He was tall, powerfully built, dressed from head to foot in black, and his expression showed nothing so much as boredom as he gazed at the girl sprawled untidily on the floor at their feet.

There was something disconcertingly familiar about his face. Not at all handsome in a conventional sense, it held something more enduring than mere good looks, a power and an aggressive sensuality, a magnetism that drew the eye despite itself. Wide Slavic cheekbones, an arresting nose with flaring nostrils that gave him the look of a highly-strung thoroughbred, at once proud and almost delicate, suggesting a subtle sensibility emphasised by the long mobile mouth, yet at the same time hinting at an exotic, perhaps savage, lineage. His lips were now clamped disdainfully together as he looked down at her. He seemed utterly un-English.

It's his bone structure, she registered automatically, and those dark, brooding eyes. He had to be East European, Hungarian perhaps, or a Cossack horseman. His eyes, dark pools with a glint of steel at the bottom of them, were fixed on her in a way that sent shivers of humiliation running up and down her spine. She was a complete fool, she read in his eyes. An ungainly mess. A disaster.

As if to confirm this impression, he lifted his head slightly and turned away. His profile was so perfect it brought tears to her eyes, and then with a sudden shock of recognition she recalled where she had seen his face before. It had been on every poster in the Underground last year. In every magazine she had happened to open. It was a shock to see him in the flesh, and no less dramatic than the intense, brooding image that had glowered out from the safety of the billboards.

Suddenly she noticed the helping hand proffered by the fair man still bending over her, and she scrambled to her feet, apologies falling from her lips as she hurriedly tried to smooth down her skirts, push back her hair, and pick up Rafe's pots of paint all at the same time.

'I'm so sorry,' she addressed the principal, red-faced with the knowledge that he would be livid over an incident like this in front of important visitors. Then she turned to Rafe. 'I haven't damaged anything, have I?' she muttered. Her face was still bright scarlet.

'Only your reputation, but don't worry, kid. At least *he's* noticed you!' Rafe gave her a wink, and started to pick up the bits and pieces.

She turned back to the visitors, but with a small nod that plainly told her she hadn't heard the last of the matter, the principal began to shepherd his guests away.

'Let me help you sort things out,' she whispered to Rafe, wanting only to hide in shame.

'It's all right. They've seen my project, and nothing's damaged anyway, so just go to your own patch. They'll be there any second.'

'God, I don't think I could face them after this!' she whispered, glancing back along the studio.

'Idiot—go on!' Rafe pushed her firmly in the right direction.

'It's Harlem Barensky, isn't it?' She nodded towards the visitors, reluctant to leave.

'Sure is.' Rafe suddenly looked rueful.

'What did he say to you?'

'Not a syllable.' Rafe looked as if he'd been mauled by a tiger, then he gave his familiar shrug. 'Not my scene anyway. I like a quiet life!'

Still flushed, Tiffany made her way as cautiously as she could towards her own workspace. The group was still talking to the girl at the next drawing desk. At least, it was the blond man who had so gallantly helped Tiffany to her feet who was doing the talking, though it was difficult to make out what he was saying. His voice rose and fell, and when he paused there was a ripple of laughter from the staff, and then Susie said something, and the man returned with a quickfire question of some sort.

Tiffany could already guess who he was. He would be the designer of Barensky's shows, one of the top theatre designers in the country. It made the rumours seem right. He must be looking for an apprentice. But why was Barensky himself here? Did he take such an interest in the day-to-day running of the company that he concerned himself with minor staff recruitment?

She bent her head over her work, dying to fiddle the little models into even more perfect alignment. In this final week of term the work on display was the accumulation of three years' hard study. There were six projects, ranging from set designs for stage plays, to a television soap and some frankly experimental work, which had thrilled Tiffany at the time but which now made her bite her lip.

She felt it was the best she had done, but she had no idea how a top professional like Frank Shore would view it, and she ran her hands nervously down the sides of her body, tucking her blouse more tightly into the wide leather belt cinching her tiny waist, checking the buttons of her blouse where they had a habit of coming undone over her voluptuous breasts, and trying to look as efficient as possible. With her glossy dark curls and smoky violet eyes, she had once been told she could look like Elizabeth Taylor.

'After extensive plastic surgery, you mean?'
she had quipped, but this morning, she had
hoped she looked fairly presentable in the
skirt of misty heather colours and the
lavender wool coat knitted by a designer
friend. Well, she needn't have bothered, she
thought glumly. Falling over like that, and
giving everyone a view of her striped
stockings and heavens knew what else!

She jerked her head nervously as the
murmur of voices became suddenly louder;
then the group were standing round her
display, and the principal was announcing
in sepulchral tones, 'Tiffany Mulgrove,' his
manner suggesting he would rather get on to
someone else as quickly as possible before
disaster could strike again. But her blond
rescuer stepped forward, charming her with
his smile at once.

'Yes, we've met already.' He smiled kindly
at her, their eyes on a level. 'You didn't hurt
yourself back there, did you?' he asked in a
friendly voice.

'Shock more than anything.' She couldn't
help smiling. He was sweet. Not at all
stuck-up, as someone so famous might have
been.

'This is Marguerite Chapman, Finance, my
right hand.' He gave her another smile, his
grey eyes expressing their evident approval
of what he saw, though whether it was her
work or her own rather dishevelled and still

flushed self she couldn't tell. Nervously she
answered his questions as fully as she could
without straying from the point.

He hadn't introduced Harlem Barensky,
and she wondered if he always stood a little
apart in that aloof manner as if everything
was really quite beneath him. It made Frank
Shore seem like some kind of front man, a
trouble-shooter, the real decisions being
made in the privacy behind Barensky's black
stare. He wasn't asking her anything, his
presence wasn't explained and he gave her
work only a cursory glance, the liquid eyes
sliding with insulting speed over the little
models it had taken so many painstaking
hours to put together.

Frank Shore was having a thorough look
at everything, though, turning from the
models to her portfolios and, after that, still
asking questions, standing for an age to
scrutinise the sketches pinned to the wall
behind her. When he turned, his friendly grey
eyes seemed no more than polite and, with a
courteous thank you, he shook her hand and
turned to the others with raised eyebrows.
'Shall we move on?'

He herded everyone out ahead of him
except Barensky, who motioned them on
then paused until the group began to move.
Then he turned to give Tiffany a searching
glance that was as unexpected as a
thousand-watt spotlight suddenly fixing her

in its glare. His eyes trailed objectively over her face, examining every nuance in its expression, registering each escaping tendril from the ill-tied velvet ribbon, the eye-shadow she was sure was smeared just from the derisory look on his face, and the blush she could not fight back. Then, with an arrogance that momentarily stopped her breath, his glance trickled slowly down to her open-necked blouse, and lingered with such telling deliberation over her breasts that she had to restrain herself from reaching up to make sure her blouse was still buttoned.

As slow as melting honey his glance oozed over the white cotton concealing her voluptuous form from view as if he could finger the softness of her breasts from across the space that separated them, and then he let his inspection slide lower to her waist, and lower still over the curving hips, and down skimming her thighs, and lower still to her feet, neatly shod in a pair of black lace-up ankle boots.

Then his dark search shifted again, moving lazily across to the sketches behind her and back to the miniature theatre sets on display, taking in herself and her life's work with no perceptible response. Then, without any sort of verbal acknowledgement, he lifted his dark head a fraction and turned, one hand reaching for the partition, using it to help him swivel away with athletic style after the others.

In a turmoil she was unable to resolve, Tiffany noticed his limp as he walked away. It didn't add any sympathy to the raging affront she felt at his silent examination. Now she understood that mauled-by-a-tiger look poor Rafe had had when she had first come in. Of course, *they* were all mere students. But did he have to make it so obvious that he held them in such blatant contempt? Some of them would be the names of the future. Given a chance. She shuddered. Her work-space seemed vast after his black shape had released her from his presence.

While the group continued on what she now saw as Barensky's royal progress through the studio, she busied herself with mental plans for the following week. One or two interviews were already lined up, though nothing really exciting had come her way yet. She wondered how long she would be out of work once the college had finished with her.

As soon as the doors had closed behind Harlem Barensky and his entourage half an hour later, the whole studio exploded into breathless gossip. Tiffany gathered that Frank Shore was apparently looking for an apprentice in his studio.

'But what the hell did that arrogant bastard have to come trailing round for?' she asked at large.

'Harlem Barensky?' It was Susie. She

pretended to mop her brow. 'What a dish! I couldn't keep my eyes off him.'

'Did he speak to you?' demanded Tiffany.

'Did he speak to anybody?' Susie looked round. Everybody was standing round the cast-iron stove in the middle of the studio, and there was a shrugging of shoulders.

'We're obviously lower than worms.' Tiffany scowled. 'I've never felt so thoroughly done over by a mere look before.' She shivered again. 'Thank God I don't have to meet *him* again!' She rubbed her hands, feeling suddenly chilled. 'I still don't understand why he condescended to look us over. Perhaps he fancied a trip to the zoo.'

'I didn't get a chance to warn you.' Rafe put his hand on her shoulder. 'He's floating a new company, independent of the national one. It's going to be his own baby. A forcing ground for new, undiscovered talent with the accent on youth.'

'Who are you quoting?' Tiffany eyed him suspiciously.

'Willie Wonka,' broke in a bearded figure next to him. 'He made an announcement shortly before Barensky arrived. It's going to be a job that'll make names. The best new dancers, the best musicians, the best artists, dress designers, choreographers. No worry about Arts Council grants. It's all privately funded. Accent on excitement, experiment and, I suspect, outrage.'

'Barensky's obviously looking for somebody to take over where he left off.' There was murmur of amused agreement, followed by a small silence.

Tiffany felt a twinge of remorse. Harlem Barensky was one of those people who shot like a meteor into the public firmament. Only the tragic accident that had crippled him, cutting short his brilliant career as a dancer, had veiled him from public view for a while. She remembered the front pages. His fight for life had been headlined for a week. Then he had pulled through, but his career was at an end. He would never dance again. Shortly after that, the film he had made in Hollywood just before the accident came out on general release, and then the whole world, more than just the dancing world, had seen what a genius had been lost. After that he had disappeared, only emerging later with a low-key guest job at the National Ballet.

His début as dance director had made his job more than a sinecure, however, for it had caused a scandal and filled the theatre night after night with the sort of people who had never before set foot in a ballet theatre in their lives. He had started to figure in the gossip columns again, taking up his meteoric private life, it seemed, just where he had left off.

With his striking looks, she could see why he had become the darling of the tabloids.

Some of the most famous beauties of the day had strewn his path. Now, having seen him for real, she could imagine how difficult it must be for him to remain out of the news even though his major claim to fame had been denied him. There was something about him that spelled power, like it or not.

'He's still an arrogant bastard,' she exclaimed, shaking out her long hair, and finally untying the useless velvet ribbon altogether. 'I pity the poor devil who gets the job!' She threw back her head. 'His side-kick's quite a sweetie, though. I wouldn't object to working with him, and if Barensky weren't involved I wouldn't mind having a shot at a job with the new company. It sounds fun!'

Just after lunch the principal sent someone down with a message, summoning Tiffany to his office. 'Oh, hell, here goes!' she murmured, trying to smarten herself up a little. 'He's going to read the Riot Act on how I've let down the college and brought ridicule on all our heads. You'd think he would be used to me by now.' It was a common joke that if anyone were going to create havoc it would be Tiffany Mulgrove. It had always been the case, even at school, and it was a frequently expressed wonder that she could turn out such painstakingly detailed designs when all around her was evidence of her knack of dropping and breaking things.

Her mother had always been her main defence, protecting her accident-prone daughter staunchly in the face of criticism. 'She's the elder of two,' she defended. 'And Fay is such a delicate, neat little thing, it's Tiffany's only way of keeping her place in the pecking order.' Amateur psychology was her mother's hobby, together with astrology. It was generally some comfort, but, as Tiffany made her way up to the office, she imagined the principal would take a rather less sympathetic view.

'Ah, Miss Mulgrove er—Tiffany.' He cleared his throat.

Now for it, thought Tiffany with an inward sigh.

He shuffled some papers then beetled a look at her from beneath grey brows. 'It seems congratulations are in order, my dear.' As she frowned in surprise he went on, 'Frank Shore was impressed by your work, and would like to see you again at a formal interview for a job as designer with Harlem Barensky's new company.'

'*Me*?' Tiffany was frankly astounded. 'But——'

'Your—er—rather unconventional entrance must have impressed him in the right way.' He chuckled and for a moment lost the air of slightly bemused formality he usually wore. 'I don't have to tell you that if you got the post it would be a real feather in our cap.'

'If I get it? You mean——'

'Naturally there will be a short list. I imagine he and Harlem Barensky have combed all the colleges for the sort of person they want.'

'And they think they might want me!' Tiffany was holding the telephone receiver so tightly it was making her hand ache. Both her parents were on the other end of the line, and she had said everything twice over. When she rang Fay later in Manchester it would be three times, and when Ginny came in it would be four. By then, perhaps, just perhaps, she might begin to believe it herself. 'What luck, isn't it?' she went on. 'Though, of course, I shan't get it. I mean, I don't know the first thing about ballet sets, but it's a real ego-boost to be short-listed. It'll keep me going as I tramp round the studios next week, Mum—Dad, I mean' she corrected as her father took over.

'Your mother's muttering something about clothes. I suppose that means you'll need something special for the interview? Who'd have daughters?' He sighed dramatically. 'I'd better pop something in the post for you tonight, hadn't I? Here, I'll hand you back to your mother.'

Before she could thank him her mother was on the line again. 'Do try to look tidy, darling. Please. I know I sound as if I'm

nagging but it is important. And after this
morning you can't afford any more mistakes.'

Tiffany was thoughtful when she replaced
the receiver. Mum's right, she realised. I'm
going to have to make a real effort this time.
The image of Harlem Barensky scudded
abruptly into her mind. Despite what she'd
said in the studio that morning, the job was
too good to throw up just because she didn't
like the look he had given her. And if she
were careful those dark eyes wouldn't get a
second chance to skim her so critically. What
she would have to do was to knock him dead
with an image of such slick, chic efficiency
that he would *have* to take her seriously. After
all, it would only match the careful,
painstaking girl locked inside the body of the
bouncy, accident-prone one he had already
met!

CHAPTER TWO

WITH her father's just delivered cheque nestling in the bottom of her wallet, Tiffany did the rounds of her favourite stores next morning, and finally came away with something so out of character that she shocked even herself. 'Black leather!' she announced to Ginny and Pat when she got back at lunchtime. 'I've had a horrible feeling all the way home in the Tube that I've made a ghastly mistake. But at least it's nothing like the soft full skirt and blouse he saw me in the first time!'

'He? Frank Shore, you mean?' Ginny gave her a glance.

'Naturally I mean Frank Shore. Who else?' Tiffany avoided her eyes. Not bothering to come up with an explanation as to why it mattered one way or the other if Frank Shore saw her in something different, she drew the black leather suit from its sheath of tissue. 'What do you think?'

'Put it on.' Pat sat back on her heels and watched as Tiffany clambered into the trousers. They were of softest black leather and fitted like a second skin.

'Smoo-ooth,' murmured Ginny as she surveyed the effect. 'Now the jacket.'

Tiffany felt the supple leather cling to her naked skin with an expensive caress that made her feel like a thousand dollars. 'Like this,' she purred, 'I feel in control.'

'I've always thought you were,' murmured Pat. 'Your clumsiness is just nerves and habit. You're not really the disaster area you seem to think.'

'You should have seen my entrance yesterday,' Tiffany remarked ruefully. 'I've never felt such a fool in my life. And Harlem Barensky obviously thought I was a complete catastrophe!'

'He'll forget all about it when he sees you in this outfit,' comforted Ginny. 'It's perfect. It gives you just the edge you need for a job with him.'

Tiffany frowned. 'I wish you wouldn't dwell on Barensky. The job is with Frank Shore, I'm relieved to say. I'll learn such a lot working in his studio if I get the job.'

'Harlem's been a heart-throb of mine ever since he left Russia to dance guest solo with the Royal Ballet,' confessed Ginny unexpectedly. 'I was twelve,' she added, 'and it was the theatrical experience of my life. If I'd known he was going to be in college yesterday you'd have seen me camping out in the corridor for a glimpse. Over in the sculpture sheds we don't hear anything that's going on, until it's too late,' she added.

Tiffany had chided Ginny for harping on

the subject of Harlem Barensky, but she had
to admit that it was with him in mind she
had chosen black. He had looked so stylish,
elegant even, in that all-male, aggressive,
exotically foreign manner, with his all-black
suit and black Russian shirt, that it was no
wonder he had women falling at his feet and
men competing to be part of his entourage.
Tiffany hadn't been able to restrain herself
from trying to emulate his style with an
all-woman version of her own.

Now she surveyed herself in the long
mirror in Pat's room and couldn't conceal
her gloom. 'I must be conceited underneath,'
she announced. 'I really imagined if I got
something slinky I'd actually look slinky. But
I'm just a short, fat woman dressed slinkily.
There's no getting away from it.'

'You're only a size twelve,' remonstrated
Ginny. 'What are you worrying about?'

'Oh, I'm slim enough for my height
everywhere but here——' she touched her
breasts '—and maybe here——' her hands
skimmed her hips '—but not even you,
Ginny, loyal though you are, would call me
feline.'

'Is that what you were aiming for?' Ginny
laughed. 'Well, you're certainly not feline, I'll
grant you, but honestly, Tiff, you're fine. Men
like comfy women. They really go for your
looks.' She glanced down at her own small
bust. 'I should know.'

But Tiffany refused to be placated. 'You don't understand. I shall be working with dancers. They'll all be as slim as laths. I'll look like Mrs Michelin next to *them*.'

'They're not slim, they're anorexic,' Pat broke in. 'And anyway, you're not a dancer, so you don't have to look like that. They want you for your designing talent, not your looks.'

'Pat, I think you're probably missing the point. She happens to be *mad* for Barensky.' Ginny gave a little cat smile.

Tiffany, peering into the mirror, grimaced at her in the reflection. 'That's right,' she said. 'I just *adore* the belittling way he looked at me on our one brief encounter. I'm *mad* to be humiliated. It really turns me on to know a guy thinks I'm a complete fool, and not worthy to live on the same planet as him.' She swung round. 'I tell you both one thing: if I ever bump into him, and he looks at me like that again, I'll do something we'll *both* regret. He made me feel short, fat, dumpy and stupid. and it was deliberate. The man's a monster!'

'I thought there'd have to be a flaw.' Ginny laughed. 'Any man with his sheer creative genius would have to be a bastard in real life. It figures!' Unconcerned, she stretched and yawned. 'Anyone for coffee?'

After she'd gone into the kitchen Pat helped Tiffany put up her hair in an elaborate style to match the sophistication of her new suit. 'What time's the interview?' she asked.

'Three-thirty at the theatre.' Tiffany glanced at her watch. 'Hours yet. But I think I'll get ready properly now, and go along in good time. You know me—I'll probably get stuck in a traffic jam, and arrive after they've all gone home.'

Her luck was running in reverse, though, and she arrived at the stage door with the realisation that she was exactly forty minutes too early. The Tube had arrived even as she'd reached the platform, and there hadn't been a single hold-up. Now she looked in vain for somewhere to wait.

After hanging round the stage door for five minutes, clutching her portfolio, she began to wonder if she dared risk losing herself in the network of East End streets around the theatre in search of a cup of coffee.

Then it started to rain. Hell, she thought. There goes my hairdo. It'll frizz up if I stay out in this. Ducking irritably through the squall, she ran up the steps to the stage door and went inside. A man behind a glass partition stopped her.

When she told him she'd got an interview with Frank Shore, he nodded and consulted a pass list. 'I know I'm early,' she apologised. 'Is there anywhere I can wait?'

'Go and sit in the Green Room, love,' he

suggested. 'There won't be anybody around
with no show on just now, but you'll be all
right.' He nodded to a door further down.
'Cut across the stage. First door in the
corridor on the other side.'

Anticipation made her heart thump
erratically as she followed his instructions
and went to the door he pointed out. It was
almost dark on the other side, with only a
dim light coming from behind some screens
and indicating the flats and pulleys overhead
to show that she was actually treading the
boards of the stage. It was more like some
furniture warehouse.

She made her way across, literally behind
the scenes, but she couldn't resist a quick
look out front. She slipped through a gap in
the flats and, with a little gasp, realised she
must be standing on the set of the last show.
Large shapes shrouded in white dust sheets
broke up the dancing space, and she
wandered about, trying to get a feel for the
scale of the set, curious to know what was
concealed beneath the covers.

If luck were on her side she would be
working with a full-scale set like this, instead
of merely making models, she told herself.
She gazed round, a sudden surge of
excitement sweeping over her as she
imagined an actual performance—she could
almost hear the excited murmuring of the
audience, the strains of the overture, the

nervous laughter of the dancers as they waited to come on stage. For the first time she knew she really wanted this job. She wanted it for what it was, for the opportunity it would bring to express all the ideas bubbling away inside her head.

She moved about the stage in a sudden daze of happiness, inspecting the way the set had been put together, already trying to learn from it how Frank Shore's design would work in practice. Then, before she could follow her curiosity further, she heard voices somewhere behind her. They were coming rapidly closer.

She froze. What would be said if she was found wandering around like this? She shouldn't even be here yet.

She crept silently to the back of the stage, intending to make her way straight to the Green Room as the doorkeeper had suggested, but something about the voices made her pause, fear at the urgent anger so close by, prickling her antennae and bringing her to a frightened halt beside one of the draped forms.

A second voice, calm and placatory, answered the first, 'It'll work out well. And if it doesn't we can change tack. What do we lose?' It was Frank Shore.

Tiffany tried to edge towards the wings, now that she had located the voices and hoped she could get out of earshot without being seen. But the first voice, the one she didn't recognise, came back loudly with words that rooted her to the spot.

'I'm right, Frank. You know I am. She's a beginner with only one thing going for her——There was a pause followed by a harsh laugh. 'Should I let you indulge yourself when it involves a risk for the company? You're wasting resources—we have no time for inefficient third-raters like Tiffany Mulgrove. I can't understand what the hell's got into you! She's not so beautiful you'd risk jeopardising the project for her, admit it. She's short and overweight. Not your type. Not my type either. A complete waste of everybody's time——'

'Hold on,' growled Frank Shore. 'There's nothing personal in all this. She's not a bad-looking kid, but that's not the point. I happen to think she's got fantastic potential——'

Tiffany didn't wait to hear the reply. As if wings were suddenly attached to her feet she flew as lightly as she could in her high heels to the edge of the stage, where thankfully her feet encountered a strip of carpet that deadened their sound, and then, holding her breath every step of the way, she practically threw herself through the door marked Green Room, closing it with a gasp behind her.

There had been no mistaking that second

voice. Its Russian accent overlaid with a transatlantic drawl was unmistakable. Besides, who else would talk to the great Frank Shore in that totally disparaging way, as if he were a fool?

Tiffany threw herself down into a chair and clutched her portfolio to her with scarcely a glance at her surroundings. What was she to do? She had come all this way for nothing. Should she walk out now, lugging her precious samples of work with her, and put the whole thing down to experience? Or should she go through the charade of an interview, knowing all the time that Harlem Barensky thought she was——She cringed inside. A complete waste of time, he had called her. The chance of a job here had receded as soon as she had heard those cruel words.

Her cheeks flushed and she rocked back and forth like a baby, desperately trying to hold back the tears. Then her fighting spirit rose up. How dared he judge her like that when he'd only given her work the most cursory glance! He might have been one of the greatest dancers for a decade, but it didn't give him the right to jeopardise her whole future with a snap judgement like that! Certainly he could persuade Frank Shore not to employ her, but he had no right to destroy her as well. And that was what his words would do if she didn't fight back!

She rose to her feet. But there was nowhere to turn. She felt trapped in the dingy little room with the shutters locked over the bar at one end and the haphazard arrangement of threadbare three-piece suites. Yet it held all her hopes, and there was nowhere she would rather have a right to be. Something had happened as she walked out on to the open spaces of the stage, and she knew it was a job she wanted to fight for if there was the least chance of getting it.

Footsteps outside alerted her, and she swivelled to face the door, every muscle tense, with no idea of how she was to face the next few minutes. Frank Shore's support would naturally have been over-ridden, and perhaps he was seeking her out now to tell her bluntly to her face she was wasting her time.

The door flew open. But it wasn't the genial fair-haired Shore who stood there. She flinched and forced herself not to step back.

For an endless moment she felt the brooding eyes of Harlem Barensky upon her. Their dark depths told her nothing of his reaction to her changed appearance. She drew herself up, still clutching her portfolio, prepared to accept his dismissal with as much hauteur as she could muster.

His face expressed nothing she could understand. It was a professional mask. Then he spoke. 'You're early, Miss Mulgrove. Is

celerity a habit of yours?' His voice was like
rough music, soft, caressing, stressing the
wrong syllables as if spoken to an inner
rhythm she had yet to learn.

Celerity, she thought frantically. What on
earth was he talking about? Pulling herself
together, she stepped forward. 'The journey
here didn't take as long as I'd expected,' she
began, her voice grown husky with the effort
of controlling the rampaging emotions his
appearance sparked off.

'Good. Then perhaps we can start?'

'Start?' She gazed at him blankly.

'The interview,' he enunciated as if to a
backward child. 'That *is* why you're here, isn't
it?'

'But I thought——' She dropped her gaze.
Now was hardly the time to tell him she'd
been eavesdropping. 'I thought my interview
was with Mr Shore.' She raised her head.

'What on earth gave you that idea? I shall
be the one employing you, not Mr Shore.' He
spoke the formal title ironically, as if unused
to hearing his colleague referred to with such
deference.

'But I'm to work in Mr—in Frank Shore's
studio?' she objected, her heart plummeting
in dismay.

'What on earth gave you that impression?
No, my dear Miss Mulgrove, if I decide you
are after all employable, you will be working
beside me in my new company. Frank

weeded you out from the others, and he naturally has a lively interest in the designs for the new company—but they will be entirely our baby.' The unexpected colloquialism sounded exotic spoken in his accent, but Tiffany was scarcely aware of it as she felt her blood slowly freeze over.

What spark of hope still remained that the job might be hers died at once. Now she knew without a shadow of a doubt that it was hopeless. If Frank Shore were to have been her potential boss then there would have been a slight chance that he could have over-ridden Harlem Barensky's objections. But now... Another fifteen minutes at the outside would see an end to this whole sorry charade. No wonder Barensky had sounded so vehement. It was at the thought of having to work with her himself.

She glanced down at her new suit. It had been an expensive and finally pointless indulgence. She couldn't imagine wanting to wear it again. It represented failure of a most wounding kind. Then, reminding herself that she still had her pride, she gave Harlem Barensky one of her coolest stares.

'Is there really any point in going on with this? Surely we could simply save your time and mine by finishing now, don't you think?'

The dark eyes narrowed, and she saw she'd shaken the aloof manner for a moment, but he recovered and came back smoothly with an arching of black brows. 'Are you suggesting I should take you on without the formality of an interview?'

She shook her head, wishing she had the courage to confirm such an unlikely suggestion.

'Then what,' he went on before she could answer, 'can you possibly mean?'

'Mr Barensky,' she began, 'isn't it obvious we could never work together?'

'Obvious to whom?' His voice was like silk, so soft she had to bend forward to catch what he was saying. 'I would hate to prejudge the issue,' he added, almost stopping her breath with the audacity of such a remark after what he had just been saying behind the scenes.

Tiffany heard herself give a strangled cry. Then, pushing her shoulders back, she moved forward, expecting him to turn and lead her to wherever the farce of an interview was to be conducted. Instead he merely leaned in the doorway, and she came to an abrupt halt about a foot in front of him, confusion momentarily mirrored in her face.

At close quarters he exuded an even stronger presence, like some kind of animal magnetism other men simply didn't possess. Feline was the word that sprang to mind. But it was no domestic pet that he resembled but a jungle animal, a panther, black as night, waiting to pounce on some innocent victim. Despite her black leather and adopted air of sophistication she felt small and helpless, and for a moment as she looked up into his eyes she knew he could see the wariness of the hunted in her face.

It was primitive. They were living in the twentieth century, but he possessed some ancient feral quality that made her think of endless Russian forests, and the broad sweep of centuries filled with passion and the rise and fall of nations. Her own life seemed dwarfed by something bigger and grander than the little concerns of her particular corner of middle-class England.

His eyes travelled interestedly over her face while these thoughts took place, and Tiffany felt a tremor rock through her body until it settled in a throbbing pulse at her temple. She wanted to gasp for air in the cool, clean outdoors, away from this overwrought backstage atmosphere, but he seemed to have no intention of moving from his position in the doorway.

'Where do you intend to interview me?' she managed to creak out.

He turned and made room for her to pass by him. 'Go up,' he told her abruptly. 'You'll have to go first. I'm afraid I take stairs tediously slowly these days.'

In spite of his accent she was impressed by his fluent English, and when she managed to focus on what he had just said she gave a start of embarrassment. His physical presence was so dominating that it was all too easy to forget his disability.

She walked up the stairs as slowly as she could, trying to match her speed to his, but he stopped for a moment half-way up and she went on, knowing the last thing he would want would be an offer of help. When he joined her at the top his bitter gaze swept her face.

'Like most cripples,' he said harshly, 'I find some days better than others.' He pushed open a door, cutting off any response she might have made, letting it bang back against the wall, and, with an abrupt gesture of his arm, indicating that she should go inside.

There was a confusion of plants and mirrors and clean green tiles inside, and then a further door opening into a room built out on to the roof of the theatre. Even from inside she could see the astonishing panorama of London spreading to the horizon. The perfect dome of St Paul's seemed to be within touching distance. She wondered if it reminded Harlem of the domes of Moscow, even though the shape was simpler.

But he was already throwing himself down on to a chesterfield with an energy that suggested he had found the stairs more difficult than even he would like to admit. 'I shall be a bad host and ask you to pour yourself a drink,' he growled, not looking at her. She gazed across, and saw that his eyes had closed for an instant. Then they flicked open, registering the sympathy that had briefly flitted over her face with unconcealed scorn. 'Well?' he snarled. 'Are you just going to stand there?'

'I can do without a drink, thank you,' she said as primly as she could.

'Well, I damn well can't. So get me one, will you?'

Carefully placing her portfolio by the door, she was half-way across the room when he called her back. 'Give it, give! Come!'

She glanced hurriedly to see what he meant, then bit her lip. He was holding out a hand towards her portfolio which she had unthinkingly placed out of reach. Hoping he didn't imagine it was deliberate, she hurried to fetch it, placing it on the chesterfield beside him and untying the strings.

'There's nothing wrong with my hands,' he snarled, glaring up at her with a baleful expression. Then suddenly he caught her eye, and his own sparked in response, lips curving. 'As you may well discover, one of these fine days,' he added in silken tones.

She gaped down at him. There was no doubt what he meant. Her anger broke its bounds and flooded to the surface. 'I understood I was not your type, Mr Barensky,' she said icily as she moved over to the drinks cabinet. Let him chew on that, she thought as she found two glasses—she'd decided she'd better have a drink, too. He hadn't replied, and when she sneaked a look across the room he gave her one long, intense glance before turning to inspect her work.

As she should have guessed, there was only vodka in the cabinet and, wishing she hadn't poured herself so much with nothing to dilute it, she returned and placed his glass within reach beside him.

'Thank you, darling.' He was preoccupied with the sketches he had spread around, and Tiffany assumed the endearment was accidental. She sat down on a gilt and brocade chair that looked as if it might have come from the Winter Palace, and watched him as warily as one would watch an untamed animal.

There was something so unpredictable about him; now he seemed almost sweet in his eagerness to see what goodies lay within the folder. Was his interest feigned, or what? she asked herself, watching him. Was this just a build-up to polite regrets? She didn't imagine he would go to such lengths to spare anybody's feelings. It made her furious that, having already made up his mind about her, he seemed to be indulging in this cat-and-mouse game, prolonging the agony to the moment when she knew she would have to get up and leave as a reject.

'Why are you frowning?' His sudden upward glance caught her unawares. Without waiting for a reply, he reached for his glass and threw back in one gulp, what she had imagined was a healthy measure, and held the glass out to her.

'You mean you want another drink?'

Her words, wrenched thoughtlessly from her as she assumed it didn't really matter what she said to him now, brought his head jerking up, dark eyes splintering with white light. 'Am I to understand you're already vetting my drinking?' He suddenly threw his head back and gave a delighted chuckle. 'What a way to begin. I should have told Frank no and meant it. I can see you're going to be nothing but trouble!' His cheekbones were even more prominent when he smiled, and she realised it was the first time she had seen anything but boredom or bitterness on that strong face. His wide mouth was still split into a grin, making the whole room come alive.

Devastated by the sudden brilliance and by the unexpectedness of what he had just said, she could only gape again.

'Be an angel, do fill it up. I feel like hell.'

She sleepwalked towards him. 'Did you say——' Realising she wasn't supposed to know what he had discussed so vehemently with Frank, she broke off, 'What did you say?' she asked finally.

'Don't be so stiff and starchy, Miss Mulgrove. Pour me a drink. And another for yourself, if you feel like it. Then come and sit down. I want to know all about these.' He tapped the sheaf of drawings with an index finger. 'You don't seem at all pleased to be working for me. Have you had a better offer?' He looked puzzled, as if trying to imagine a better offer than the one he was making.

Feeling faint, Tiffany simply shook her head. Maybe she did need another drink. One thing was sure—she didn't know which was worse, Harlem Barensky as predator, or the possibly more dangerous man who was now laughing across at her with a smile that could only be described as gorgeous lighting his whole face.

And as for not seeming pleased to be working for him—what on earth was she to make of a statement like that?

CHAPTER THREE

TIFFANY declined his invitation to sit next to him and remained safely at a distance on the gilt and brocade chair, clutching her glass hard as if for protection. 'Mr Barensky,' she managed to croak at last, 'am I working for you?'

'Don't you want to?' he riposted, raising his eyebrows in mock astonishment.

Tiffany tactfully ignored that, and said, 'You seemed to have doubts about me.'

'Perceptive and true,' he replied with a disarming smile, 'But Frank thinks you're the most interesting talent he's seen for some time—I quote, of course—and as I've always found his judgement to be most sound I'm quite happy to give it a whirl, as they say.'

'A temporary appointment?'

'Everything in this world, Miss Mulgrove, is temporary.' For a moment his eyes darkened, and his lips curved in a bitter smile. Then he leaned back, one hand keeping his place in her portfolio, and asked, 'Are you turning me down?'

'No, no, of course not——' Tiffany blurted out, confused by the sudden thought that perhaps it would be safer if she did so. 'I just thought——'

'I probably gave you the idea I wasn't impressed by you?'

A master of understatement! She nodded, not trusting herself to speak.

'Quite right,' he agreed. 'I'm not. I don't like lateness, inefficiency, sloppiness, clumsiness or——' he glanced down at the folio '—deceit or lack of talent.' His face was like granite now, swept of any warmth. He tapped one of the sketches. 'This *is* all your own work, I presume?'

Colour scalded her cheeks. 'Of *course* it is!' Before she could unleash a tirade in response to his insulting insinuation, he held up a hand.

'OK. Cool it!' He gave her an amused smile. 'You must forgive me—I don't deal in polite word games. And maybe I don't know your language well enough to express what I want to say?'

'It seems to me you know my language very well,' she broke in, unable to contain herself any longer. 'You're accusing me of copying someone else's ideas——'

'Not at all. I was asking, not accusing. Sometimes students absorb influences excessively, sometimes deliberately, sometimes without realising it. This group, for instance—' he riffled through the sheets until he came to a batch of early drawings '—the Bauhaus influence is very strong here . . .'

'I know it is. We were set an exercise and I

fulfilled its requirements. I put it in because I think it's a practical solution to the problem we were set.' She stopped abruptly, her mind going blank, and clamped her lips in a straight line to stop them trembling, resisting the impulse to down her drink in one gulp. The black leather had softened with her body heat, and she was suddenly aware of its touch against her skin. Her breasts seemed to be pressing tightly against the confining leather in a way that was distracting her from what she was trying to say. Even sitting on the other side of the room the dark shape of Harlem Barensky seem to bulk too large, dwarfing her with its colossal presence. She forced herself to keep very still and concentrate.

He turned back to the folder and riffled through it again. 'We'll leave all that for now. I notice you have here only one or two designs for dance shows. Does that mean the dance doesn't interest you?'

'It's not something I'd thought about specialising in, if that's what you mean,' she admitted candidly. 'Most theatre work is for drama. Jobs with ballet or opera companies are few and far between. I have to think of the future.'

'But you have no prejudice against the dance?'

Why does he keep calling it 'the dance'? she wondered. 'Ballet isn't anything I'm

prejudiced against, no,' she told him politely.
'Nor can I confess to knowing much about
it, either,' she added, to be on the safe side.

'Very diplomatic. I suppose you're trying to
tell me you'll take anything that comes your
way?'

'Not quite anything, Mr Barensky.' She
lifted her chin. 'But I'm a professional, or at
least I shall be as soon as I leave college next
week——'

'It takes a lifetime to become a
professional, my dear Miss Mulgrove,' he cut
in smoothly, his enigmatic glance sliding
over her. 'Don't imagine it's something that
happens overnight. You'll be an apprentice
for many years. As a complete beginner
you're going to need to take all the advice
you can get.'

'I understand that,' she replied coolly, 'but
I also have ideas of my own. Isn't that why
Mr Shore picked me out from the rest?'

He gave her a silvery glance. 'Let us hope
that was his prime reason.' He snapped the
folio shut, stretched out his long legs in front
of him and rested his head on the back of
the chesterfield, closing his eyes as if sinking
into some alien world inaccessible to her.
Tiffany couldn't help letting her eyes dwell
more fully on him now, after the darting and
accidentally colliding looks that had just
preceded. His face expressed a haunting
sadness in repose, but she noted too its harsh

virility, and the flagrant sensuality of his lips.
When he smiled he changed into a daemon,
a Pan, a Bacchus. The image mixed headily
with the Cossack horseman she had
glimpsed during their first encounter.

She thought he was tired, leaning back like
that as if sinking into a sleep state, but she
should have known his mind was working
actively behind the façade of repose for,
without opening his eyes, he began to speak.

'I admit I was mystified by you when I saw
you in college,' he began slowly. 'What a mess
you were! I couldn't reconcile your
appearance with those rather appealing,
delicate, intricate, very sound little structures
you were supposed to have made . . . of
course, their appeal for Frank is their surreal
imagery—and their gaucheness, perhaps——'

'Gauche?' she exclaimed, so loudly it made
his eyes snap open. So her entrance had been
a mess, all right; she would give him that. But
gauche? That was too much!

'Is that the right word?' he asked
disarmingly before she could say anything
and, grinning at her fiery face, he added,
'Perhaps I mean freshness?'

'You *said* gauche——'

'Well, yes, that's true. Perhaps a little of
that, no?' He raised black eyebrows.
'Inevitably,' he added as if to himself before
she could disagree. 'Just like you yourself, in
fact. Your lovely black leather makes you

look sleek and sophisticated, Miss Mulgrove,'
he went on swiftly, narrowing his eyes at her,
'but underneath I suspect there remains the
frightened, confused little girl I saw yesterday . . . sprawling so charmingly on the floor
at my feet with her knickers showing.'

Tiffany gasped. Then she jerked back her
head with the glass to her lips. When she
leaned sideways to replace the empty glass
on a side table her hands were trembling.
Harlem Barensky was laughing softly.

'I think that rather proves my point, doesn't
it?'

'What proves your point?' she asked in a
stiff voice, not looking at him.

'You're so easily disconcerted.' He seemed
to move closer but it was only his voice that
changed. 'Keep cool, Miss Mulgrove. There
will inevitably be worse to come.'

'Worse?' she stuttered.

'Life is like that.' His expression was harsh,
and she knew all at once that underneath the
deliberate banter there was a bitterness like a
solid stratum of black rock in the man's soul.

'Get me another drink, and let's get to
work,' he said abruptly.

'To work?' She couldn't keep track of him.

'No time like the present. Isn't that what
you say?'

'Personally, no, Mr Barensky. I try to avoid
clichés.'

'In actions as well as words, Miss

Mulgrove?'

Not sure what he meant, she thought it wiser to nod.

'And would you regard it as a cliché of action if I asked you to come over here and sit next to me?'

'It would only become a cliché, Mr Barensky, if——' She bit her lip, wondering whether she dared say what she'd intended.

'If I put my arm around you and accidentally kissed you, for instance?'

She gulped and nodded.

'Well, let's avoid cliché at all costs. But we can have another drink at least, surely?'

Numbly she rose from her seat and walked over to the cabinet. The movement was a brief respite from being within the orbit of his attention. She felt frazzled, every cell of her body jumping in chaos.

'I hope you like vodka. It's our company drink.' She swung with a little gasp. He was standing right behind her and must have moved with the stealth of a panther. 'Yes, I can walk,' he murmured, misinterpreting her sharp intake of breath. 'It's dancing I can't do any more. That's all.' His lips twisted cynically. 'So that's all right, isn't it?'

She found herself pressing against the rosewood and gilt drinks cabinet behind her, her breath held in, the hair at the nape of her neck erect with some emotion she couldn't name.

'Mr Barensky——' she began, putting up a hand in defence. Then her nerves shrieked as a telephone bell splintered the brief tension between them.

He swung away, but not before she'd seen a gleam of light behind the dark lashes which showed his appreciation of the irony of being interrupted at that precise moment. He was just about to kiss me, thought Tiffany wildly. I can't let him. He's too . . . She gulped, frantically trying to steady her nerves. He's too everything, she thought, turning to look across the room.

He was leaning against the arm of the chesterfield, an old-style ebony-black telephone in his hand, talking rapidly to someone in Russian. His voice rose and fell, and only when he gave a smoky laugh did she suspect that the caller might be a woman.

She poured a drink for him and a tiny one, to calm her nerves, for herself, and was about to sit down again when he clicked his fingers to attract her attention. He was still speaking rapidly into the phone, but one hand waved out and, interpreting, she went over to place his glass in it, wondering if he always drank at this rate and whether it was a requirement of the job that she join in. Already she felt dazed, though whether it was entirely due to the unaccustomed alcohol midway through the afternoon she wouldn't have liked to guess.

His conversation seemed interminable, and while she waited she toyed with the idea of turning down the job after all. He was going to be hell to work with and she didn't fancy being swallowed in, mangled up and spat out when no longer useful.

She gave him a covert glance, trying to assess whether the ruthlessness she saw in his face, the sudden cruel curve of the lips, the bitterness were real, and if so whether they made his dazzling smile, like the sun breaking in splendour from behind a mountain crag, any less real.

She pushed a hand over her brow. It was time to take a grip on herself. He was right when he said she was gauche. He was only a man, for heaven's sake. Famous—OK. Wildly sexy—without doubt. But after that just the same as anybody else. It was crazy to let her feelings run mad like this. What was more, he was going to be her employer. And the biggest cliché of all was to carry a torch for the boss. She disavowed cliché, thank you very much. She was an individual, original and—what else had Frank Shore called her? The most interesting talent he had come across for some time?—and she couldn't afford to lose her grip. She wasn't the type to let a lethal smile sabotage her future.

The telephone conversation seemed to go on endlessly. She managed to drag her eyes away from him and take a proper look around the room.

It was a mixture, to say the least. Alongside the Winter Palace cast-offs were two very English leather chesterfields, an enormous wall mirror in a massive gilt frame circled with cherubs and coronets—a throw-out from Versailles?—and a collection of straight-backed dining chairs round an Italian marble table in pale greys and soft pinks. The chairs looked American, beautiful, functional, high-tech stuff and somehow fitting in perfectly with the rest of the décor. A huge hand-woven tapestry warmed the room with its mixture of hot pinks and reds and blues and, although it was late afternoon now with the sky filtering in a pale midsummer wash of colour through the terrace windows, she could imagine that when the lamps were lit it would be cosy and inviting. A secret hideaway among the silvery geometric shapes of London roofs.

Her eye picked out a collection of photographs on the table beside her, and she smiled slightly at one of a small boy in a white tunic self-consciously holding a garland of roses. There was another one, the same boy, a year or two older, in the black velvet jacket and tights of a ballet dancer, performing a quite perfect *jeté*.

Then she leaned forward. That wide mouth was unmistakable. A glance at the other photographs in the collection showed her they were all of Harlem Barensky at various ages and dancing different roles. He looked so in character for each one, assuming each role with the chameleon quality of an actor, that only the expressive mouth betrayed his identity.

She peered closer. The latest one seemed to be a Hollywood shot taken on set. It must have been shortly before the accident. It showed a handsome, tanned man in a white suit in his early thirties, the awareness of having the world at his feet vivid in his eyes. Next to that there was a studio shot taken at the age of eighteen or so, the man's maturity already hinted at beneath the gentle lines of the boy's face, as he tenderly held a young girl in his arms—she was exquisite in a cloud of white tulle. Such an ethereal exchange had passed between them both as the camera clicked that Tiffany felt a pang at the thought of first love, lost love. Her own first love had been for a boy who lived at the end of the street. They had once held hands, and for years afterwards she had remembered the exact date with nostalgic fondness. She couldn't prevent the stray thought that questioned whether Harlem Barensky's first love had been so innocent despite the girl's chaste look and air of fragility.

'So you've found the collection.' Suddenly he was standing over her in the flesh, and she had to concentrate to get the photograph to stand up properly as she replaced it.

'I'm sorry, I hope you don't mind,' she blurted.

'Therapy, not vanity,' he said bluntly. 'I'm told if I can bear to contemplate the past without wanting to tear down the walls I'll know I've come through. Do you believe that?' His black eyes swivelled to her and she felt them tear to shreds all possible polite replies, boring into her as if to drag a response from the very recesses of her soul. Unprepared for such a ruthless appraisal, she felt her mind go blank, then, assuming he was talking about the accident that had crippled him, she said cautiously, 'It would depend on your attitude. Whether you're ready to let the past go and start anew. I've never been in a serious accident so I can only guess what it must be like.'

'What? The accident-prone Miss Mulgrove has never pranged her car?'

'I don't drive. And, anyway, what makes you say I'm accident-prone?' She gave a nervous glance at the spindly table on which the photographs were arranged.

'The principal of your college——' he told her.

'He said that?' she burst out.

So much for loyalty, she was thinking, when he went on, 'He happened to be defending your catastrophic entrance. He seemed to find it rather endearing, part and parcel of your impetuous talent. I quote, of course.' He wasn't smiling, though his words were said lightly, almost pleasantly. His tone hardened, though, when he told her, 'I'm afraid I don't share his penchant for disorder. I have no rules here, Miss Mulgrove, bar one. I will not tolerate carelessness. I have no time for people who are slack, people who don't know their job, people who let things slip by out of sheer laziness. In that sense you'll have to be a professional from head to toe the minute you step in here. Am I making myself clear?'

'Perfectly.' She felt her glance locked by the fierceness of his stare.

'Safety comes first in this theatre. I want no accidents. No mistakes. Your designs must not only fulfil their artistic function, they must make the safety of my dancers their priority.'

'I shall try to do my best——' she began.

'I don't award gold stars for trying, Miss Mulgrove.' He regarded her with a look of misgiving and added, 'The gold stars are for success only. And let me tell you, it's got to be one hundred per cent every time? Understand?'

She couldn't tear her eyes away from the grim lines of his face. There was no knowing what made him so uncompromising, but she faced him squarely and, without flinching beneath his stare, replied, 'You're the boss, Mr Barensky and I'll go along with whatever you say.' She gave a little gasp and added hurriedly, 'I mean, whatever conditions you impose——' This sounded little better and she forced herself to stop talking.

'I sincerely hope you're not as muddle-headed as you sound.' His expression was full of doubt, and he glanced across the room at the scattered drawings. 'Why don't you pick them all up and put them away? I want you to listen to a little music with me.' While he went over to an elaborate sound system built into the wall units she did as he suggested, wondering what the purpose of the invitation was when he'd already told her he wanted them to start work now.

Would it be Tchaikovsky she would have to endure? Not that she didn't like his ballet music, but it was swirly, romantic stuff, as far as she could remember, and she could imagine the effect of that on her nerves if she had to sit in touching distance of Harlem Barensky for the rest of the afternoon!

He may be hell, she thought, but she couldn't deny the melting effect he had on her body. It must have been what came over the footlights when he danced. Charisma, sheer animal magnetism, the primeval call of male to female . . . She shut off thoughts like this as she felt him take the portfolio from her hands and watched him place it on the floor beside them. Then she felt him pull her down beside him among the cushions as the first strains of music trickled into the dimly lit room.

CHAPTER FOUR

'I GOT the job!' Tiffany raced up the stairs and into the kitchen where she knew Ginny and Pat would be, pausing only to throw her portfolio through the open door of her bedroom before turning to watch their expressions. Satisfied she had their attention, she disappeared again.

'I'm just getting changed,' she called, already stripping off the black leather suit and hanging it roughly inside her wardrobe. Both girls came clustering into her room. 'He told you there and then you were in? Lucky old you. They usually keep you waiting ages!' exclaimed Pat. 'When do you start?'

'I've started.' She threw a glance at her drawing-block on the bed. 'I go in properly tomorrow morning.' The memory of Harlem Barensky's husky voice saying, just before she left, 'I want you tomorrow . . .' with that double edge of innuendo, made her blush. As she drew up a pair of track-suit bottoms, she added, 'But I'm not working for Frank Shore.'

'What?' Ginny studied her face. 'I thought you'd just had an interview with him?'

Tiffany shook her head, pulling on a sweatshirt, her face a mixture of happiness

58

and hysteria. She knew just what Ginny's reaction was going to be. Playing up to it, her arms spread wide, she announced, 'I'm working for your hero, Ginny . . . Mr Cossack Horseman . . . Ivan the Terrible . . . Macho Man himself!'

'Who? You don't mean . . .? Never Barensky? No! I don't believe it!'

'Neither did I. I'm still telling myself it's a horrible dream!'

Ginny ignored Tiffany's last remark and grasped her by both arms, swirling her about the room. 'You've got to let me come in with you one day, Tiff. Please! You've simply got to! Is he heaven close to? What's he like? Tell me! How tall is he in real life? Oh, Tiff, you must tell me. You are lucky!'

Tiffany disengaged herself and flopped down across her bed, 'I knew you'd react like this.' She wasn't smiling now. When she raised her head Ginny stopped waltzing about and gave her a closer look.

'Isn't everything all right. What's the matter?'

Tiffany sat up, and ticked off the points one by one on her fingers. 'He thinks I'm gauche, useless and a complete waste of time. He also thinks my appearance is a complete mess, and my designs likely to fall down and kill all his dancers in mid-flight. In addition, he seems to be labouring under the fond delusion that I'm a complete push-over and in danger of succumbing to his rather obvious Russian charm. I worked that last one out on the Tube coming home,' she added quickly, remembering the curt way he had dismissed her as soon as the tape had finished. To Ginny's and Pat's protests she said, 'He also admits to not wanting to employ me at all and is only doing so to appease Frank Shore, whose opinion he actually confesses to respecting——'

'If he's the type who's willing to appease people, he can't be too bad. So what does he think about your actual work?' cut in Ginny briskly.

Tiffany blushed. 'Actually he seems to think it might do. Apparently, it's surreal enough to appeal to Frank Shore so he's willing to go along with it for now.'

'And Frank Shore?'

'I didn't meet him this time, worse luck. He seemed quite sweet that day in college and I discovered he thinks, quote, I'm not a bad-looking kid, have fantastic potential and am the most interesting talent he's seen for some time, unquote.'

'Wow! That's neat!'

'He told you that?' asked Pat, impressed.

'No, I regret to say I overheard most of it when he was defending me to Barensky who, I might add, violently disagreed. It was all a muddle. I shouldn't have overheard them anyway, it was an accident, and I wanted to

walk out there and then.' She rolled over on
the bed. 'It was awful. For a minute I didn't
know what to do. It sounded as if I hadn't
got a chance, but Barensky himself came in
before I could escape. And, anyway, even if
I'd been able to escape, I would probably
have stayed because, oh, listen, you two!' She
sat up. 'I really do want the job. The theatre's
a gem and it could be so wonderful. He's
getting some fantastic people to work for
him——'

'Wait a minute, let's get this straight. You
sound a bit muddled . . .'

'That's another thing he said about me. I'm
muddle-headed.' Tiffany stopped trying to
make sense, and gave them both a distraught
glance. 'What am I going to do? I can't work
with anybody who thinks I'm so, so useless,
can I?'

'There, there, I'm not surprised you're in a
state. He's dynamite on stage. What on earth
he's like close to . . . in the flesh?' Ginny gave
a little shiver, and Pat shrugged.

'I'm dying to meet this guy,' she said. 'He
sounds too good to be true!' She went to the
door. 'While you two drool over him I'll go
and brew up. Then I'll lend you, Tiffany, a
book on positive thinking.' As she went out
she added lugubriously, 'I guess this is the
only good news to hit this house for months.'

Ginny frowned. 'Pat's still waiting to hear
whether she's got that interior design job

she's after. It's been nearly a week. She's out of her mind. But listen, Tiff, what's all the wailing for? You're in with a peach of a chance and that's all that matters.'

'But, and I quote, "Everything in this world, Miss Mulgrove, is temporary."' She wrinkled her brow. 'You know what that means? If I fail to please the master I'm out on my ear. And what if I've turned down a safer job in the meantime?'

'Risky. But that's life. There's no reason why he should throw you out, is there? If Frank Shore picked you out you can be sure you've got a good chance of hacking it.'

'Frank Shore and Harlem Barensky are two entirely different people. *Entirely* different,' Tiffany repeated feelingly. She hugged her knees. 'Seriously, Ginny, I'm not sure I can handle it.'

'Him, you mean?' asked Ginny shrewdly.

Tiffany nodded. 'It's been the worst afternoon of my life. I don't know where I am.'

'I gather he's as gorgeous in the flesh as on film, then?' Ginny curled on the rug beside Tiffany's bed.

'Gorgeous? Can that be an understatement?' she asked with a shaky laugh. 'He's six foot one of pure male. He looks like magic. And his voice makes my toes curl. But as a man to work for . . . with . . . by the side of . . . Ginny, he's too much. I can't!'

'You know you can.'

Tiffany nodded. 'It's going to be like walking over a minefield. One false move and he'll blow me apart.'

Next morning she rang the college, formally asked if she could skip the last week of term and listened with a detached smile to her head of department's unfeigned delight that she'd landed such a plum job. She'd probably be back before the week was out, ego in tatters, but she couldn't spoil his sense of achievement by telling him so. 'Thanks for all your help these last three years, Reg. I'll try and get time off to come in on the last day of term to say goodbye to you all.'

She arrived at the theatre at nine sharp with what she hoped was noticeable celerity. It had been a problem to decide what to wear on her first day. Country-house skirts that might reveal her knickers again if she happened to fall over, she thought wryly, were out. The black leather was too expensive for every day. So she settled on a practical outfit of twill slacks with a loose smock top in the same hazy violet as her eyes. She wanted to pass unnoticed, but at the same time not look so dowdy that it damaged her about-to-be-dented ego.

The stage doorman greeted her with a friendly smile. 'He's on set, Miss Mulgrove.

Go right in.'

Thanking him, she made her way down the now familiar corridor and pushed the door into the wings. It still looked like a furniture warehouse, she thought, as she stumbled in the gloom behind the flats. The same piece of music as he had played for her the previous day, the theme for the first piece she was to work on with him, filled the space with its haunting melody, the twelve-bar rhythm and blues guitar played by a top American artist wrenching at her emotions yet again.

Hardly Tchaikovsky, she had thought the first time she'd heard it, and she had thrilled to realise that Barensky's new company was going to be everything it was reported to be—up-to-the-minute hot shoe, with young appeal, a future public sensation.

Suddenly she found herself in a blaze of light from the single spot. Momentarily blinded, she moved out of it, and became aware of a figure in black sitting on a chair in the middle of the stage down front. Lit by the spill-out from the light, his face was awash with shadow, but the shape and slump of the broad shoulders suggested it was Harlem Barensky himself. He was alone.

Blue Monday, she thought, moving soundlessly across the stage in her rubber-soled trainers, unaware that he hadn't noticed her arrival until she drew almost level with him. She came to a hesitant stop when he didn't

acknowledge her presence. Something about
his deep stillness made her hold her tongue.
He looked lost in thought. Blocks of shadow
sculpted his face, his sensual lips curving in
a picture of bitterness. The riveting eyes with
their suddenly live, silver flashes were concealed in deep shadow, but she could guess
their expression was moody, like the taped
blues sound filling the theatre.

Not sure how to approach him after his
curt dismissal of her yesterday as soon as the
tape had come to an end, she waited now
until the melody line finished, then stepped
forward. On cue he lifted his head.

'Very sensitive, Miss Mulgrove. I'm glad
you know how to listen. Drag up a chair and
let's begin.' His dark eyes glittered wickedly
through the shadows, confounding her
suspicion of moodiness, and she swayed
under their electric impact as they connected
violently with her own. She took a deep
breath and walked carefully to the side of the
stage, picked up a straight-backed wooden
chair and returned with it, placing it two feet
away from his own.

'A little closer, if you please. I don't want
to be forced to shout at this stage.' He gave
her a panther's smile from which she turned
with a jerk of her head, edging her chair an
inch closer and dragging a drawing-block
from her case, snapping it shut with an air
of deliberate efficiency.

'Good morning, Mr Barensky,' she said, as if reproving him for his lack of conventional greeting. It was best if she began as she meant to go on. And at arm's length was the best place to keep him.

His ferocious concentration kept them both at work till late morning without a break. Her notes overflowed the pages, a mixture of words and phrases and lightning sketches. The way he described the piece she could see it already in her imagination. It was going to be dynamite. Just like him. His own ideas sparked off hers and vice versa, and when he suggested a break she was as breathless as if she'd been riding a roller-coaster. Reluctantly she lifted her pen.

'We're having lunch with the rest of the team so you can get to know them. Afterwards Frank will allot you a corner of his studio so you can get down to work right away. We'll meet again tomorrow morning, by which time I hope you'll have plenty to show me.'

'Right.' She closed her drawing-block with a satisfied slap. 'Thank you, Mr Barensky. That was all very helpful.'

She picked up her bag and rose to go, but a hand detained her, touching her softly but firmly, the contact melting her bones and sweeping away all her self-composure in an instant. Submitting to his touch as if it were nothing, she raised her eyebrows.

'Only one thing more,' he suggested softly. 'I notice you called him Frank earlier——'

'I'm sorry,' she broke in. 'I didn't mean any disrespect. If you'd rather I called him Mr Shore——'

'I'm sure he would soon correct me if I insisted on such an out-of-date formality.' He gave that smoky laugh she had heard before, and his fingers tightened round her wrist. 'What I'm trying to suggest, Tiffany, is that you relax a little and try using first names. Call me Harlem, right?'

'I—yes, of course, Mr—Harlem.'

'If it's too much to ask——' he released her wrist '—I won't sack you because you insist otherwise . . .'

'I'll try to remember . . . Harlem.'

'OK.' His glance was surprisingly gentle. 'I'm frequently told I'm a bastard slave-driver. If it gets too much, yell. We're working as a team. That means you can call the shots some of the time.'

'I'll—I'll try to remember,' Tiffany said, biting her lip and unable to attract the lightness to her voice that his words invited. It was the touch of those warm fingers on her bare skin. In time she would get used to the accidental brush of them. It was the novelty of it that was getting to her. The tingling of her body right now was all due to her former antagonism, nothing else.

But, as he had warned the day before, there

was worse to come. 'Would you be an angel,' he asked as she turned away, 'and give me the loan of your shoulder for a minute?'

Puzzled, she looked down, her senses momentarily swamped by the implications of such a request.

'All I mean is—here.' He reached out for her arm. 'I'm sorry.' He struggled to his feet, leaning heavily on her for a moment and avoiding her glance, his mouth set in a harsh horizontal that showed how much he hated his disability.

'It's all right,' she said briskly. 'I'm stronger than I look. Lean as much as you need to.' Their faces were on a level and he turned, the effort of getting to his feet showing clearly in his eyes. She saw the grooves of pain on either side of his mouth deepen; then he stood upright, for a moment looming over her, one arm still hooked round her waist.

'They tell me it'll be easier than this eventually. I can't wait. Not that they know what the hell they're talking about. I know a damned sight more about it than they do by now.'

'I'm sure you do,' she agreed, taking his weight for a moment longer than necessary. He felt her continued support and gave a wry smile.

'I thought for a minute you were going to start preaching at me, as you did yesterday about my drinking.' He patted her hand and moved away.

She took a shaky step after him, but in the sudden confusion his touch had wrought forgot that she still held her case under one arm and, too late, felt it slither to the floor. It burst open with the impact, scattering papers and pens and drawing inks all over the stage.

'Hell,' she muttered, flying to gather them all together. She gave a hurried glance and saw he was leaning on his stick, grinning down at her.

'The disastrous Miss Mulgrove,' he murmured ironically. 'I'm really going to have to keep a strict eye on you, aren't I?'

'It won't happen again, I——' Hastily she crammed everything back into the bag and straightened up, flinching as his bright glance raked her face.

He laughed softly. 'I'll find it quite encouraging to be working with somebody even more clumsy than myself. And watching your continual confusion will be an occupation with a delight all its own.'

He held out an arm for her to take. 'Come along, child. I'll make allowances this once.'

Relieved to find his mood mellow rather than the reverse, she looped her arm in his, lending support. 'Your accident happened about a year ago, didn't it?' she asked, matching her pace with his as they made their way towards the wings.

He nodded.

'It's early days, then.'

'They said complete rest for a year. Damned fools. Can you credit it?' He raised his eyebrows in disbelief. 'I told them what I thought of that suggestion.' Tiffany could imagine in what terms he had made his opinion known, too. She gave a laugh.

When they came to the door leading out into the corridor he paused for a moment, this time leaning heavily against the door for support and successfully barring her way. 'Tell me, do you think it diminishes my effectiveness in any way?' His tone was self-mocking, but when she looked into his face she detected a deeper pain concealed beneath the apparent lightness of the question.

'I don't know how effective you were before,' she replied, choosing her words carefully and deliberately avoiding the ambiguity of the question. 'But, if it's any comfort, Lord Byron didn't seem to have many problems.'

'Byron?' He laughed aloud. 'That's a good one. I'll have to remember that.'

'So long as you don't keep a pet bear in the theatre too!'

'Is that what he did?'

'So they say. Dogs and cats were forbidden in university rooms, so he got round the rules by buying a bear.'

Harlem was still chuckling, but the old bitterness came back all of a sudden and he grunted, 'I'm the performing bear here, aren't I? A Russian bear. Is that what you meant?'

Tiffany flushed and stared him straight in the eye. 'Mr Barensky——' she began, before hurriedly correcting herself '—Harlem, I would never . . .' She stopped, reining in her momentary anger that he could imagine she'd meant to imply such a thing. She went on more gently. 'You can't think I meant that. I suppose it's my own fault, though. I keep forgetting you find it difficult to get about, and I suppose I might have given the wrong impression. I'm sorry, Harlem,' she said, and asked softly, 'Have I been thoughtless?'

'On the contrary, you've been wonderfully considerate.' He opened the door and prepared to go on. 'I just wanted to know what you felt. I guess you've told me clearly enough.' He didn't elaborate, but went on, 'I'm a lousy invalid and still find it impossible to believe everything's over. It's my damned Achilles tendon,' he told her. 'Nothing to be done about it.'

'Byron knew that, too,' she told him, taking his arm without his asking her to.

'I'll remember that.' He gave her a wide smile, his mouth on a level with her forehead, and for a second time she felt an overwhelming conviction that the expression in those slightly slanting eyes meant he was thinking of kissing her. Again something stopped him, this time in the shape of Frank Shore who was just coming in from the street.

'Tiffany, lovely to meet you again, my dear. I gather he's started slave-driving already?'

'That's a loaded question, Mr Shore——' she began, confused to feel Harlem's arm weighing heavily round her waist, but Frank Shore didn't seem to notice or, if he did, he put it down to the fact that Harlem needed physical help. Now he put out his own arm.

'Here, Harlem. Let's go. I've got the car outside. Lana and the others are already on their way. Come along, Tiffany,' he said. 'Time for lunch.'

The two men went on ahead and Tiffany followed. There was plenty to think about as she watched them make their way into the street. For one thing the morning had raised her spirits magnificently. It really seemed as if she and the great Harlem Barensky were going to be able to work together in perfect harmony. And now that she was getting to know him better her earlier opinion could be revised somewhat. He might be a slave-driver, but he was sensitive too, with a sense of humour that made any festering antagonism unlikely. All she had to control was the effect his touch had on her, of making her body tingle all over. It might not be the sign of antagonism that she had first thought, and if that were so then the minefield she had mentioned to Ginny was going to be really dangerous to negotiate. Confident in her new happiness that she could handle it, she stepped out into the sunlight and made her way to the waiting car.

The restaurant the inner group of the company had made their own was a Russian place in one of the East End backstreets. Tiffany was surprised when Frank's gleaming silver Jaguar drew up outside its rather nondescript entrance and, while he went to find a parking spot on a piece of open land nearby, she cast an interested eye over the menu outside. Half was in Cyrillic, half in a perfunctory, pencilled-in English translation

'I hope you like stew?' Harlem asked as they waited for Frank outside. 'They understand us here and don't object to feeding an army of starving dancers at any time, day or night.'

'I didn't think dancers ate much anyway,' she remarked.

'Don't kid yourself. They eat like horses. All that jumping about!' He grinned. 'They're a tough crowd with the stamina of navvies. You wouldn't be the first one to be taken in by the ethereal façade!'

Silently she observed his broad shoulders, imagining the bulging pectorals straining beneath the cloth jacket, and couldn't help giving a little smile.

Frank came up then and helped Harlem through the door. They were both greeted with open arms by the proprietor, who quickly turned to Tiffany and shook her warmly by both hands when Frank told him who she was. There was a delicious aroma coming from a back kitchen, and a noisy group at two tables pushed together in the middle of the room told her that the other members of the company had already arrived.

Feeling a little out of place to begin with, she soon felt her spirits warm as they welcomed her as if she'd been working with them for ages. Harlem was obviously adored by everybody, male and female alike, and Tiffany couldn't help noticing the seductive smiles his principal dancer, Svetlana, kept throwing in his direction from across the table. Frank asked him to translate the menu for her, and when their order arrived she saw immediately what he had meant—whatever name it went under, the food was basically lashings of meat and potatoes, with several enormous communal platters groaning with vegetables.

'So much for Russian salad,' observed Tiffany to Marguerite opposite, as her plate was piled high, and she wondered how quickly she was going to put on weight if she ate with the company every day.

Harlem was watching her expression with amusement. 'You can always say no,' he observed with a sly smile. 'Or would that be against your principles, perhaps?'

Aware of a double meaning but unsure whether that had been in his mind, she joked, 'I often say no, as you'll probably find out.' That should put paid to the idea I'm a push-over, she thought, avoiding his amused glance.

Casting a swift eye round the table as they ate and talked, she couldn't help wondering what Harlem's private relationships with these people were. Lana was beautiful, in a skinny, dagger-smart sort of way, with elongated cat's eyes and a crushing elegance that made Tiffany feel clumsy and fat. Marguerite, the company accountant, was smart too, with a clear, enamelled gloss that was pure sophistication. Tiffany could imagine either woman being the perfect adornment for Harlem's arm. Of the men, Maurice was obviously the star, his slow, muscular movements confirming what Harlem had told her about the physical shape of his dancers. In an open-necked shirt straining over broad shoulders, Maurice could have just walked in off a building site. He was keeping his end of the table amused with an account of a recent tour he had done with another company.

'Confusing, isn't it?' Frank observed,

lowering his head. 'I'd have to go back fifteen years or so to recall my first job with a crowd like this. But I love it. It gets to you—the slog of rehearsals when nothing ever seems to go right, then the furore of the first night, everybody's nerves at breaking point, then the euphoria afterwards when you know you've made friends and changed lives. Think you'll want to stay?'

Tiffany nodded with unexpected fervour. 'If you'll have me,' she told him, 'I certainly will.'

She felt Harlem stir beside her, distracted from the conversation he was having across the table with Marguerite, and he turned at the same moment she did, his dark eyes washing over her in quizzical appraisal. She saw his lips tighten momentarily before he turned back again to finish what he had been saying. Disturbed by the intensity of that shadowed glance, she put it down to a misunderstanding of what she and Frank had been talking about. She couldn't guess what thought had skidded through his mind, but whatever it was he didn't seem to like it. A return of her first forebodings made her bite her lip. He wasn't an easy man. There was something black within him that revealed itself at unexpected moments like a shoal under the surface of a storm-swept sea. It made him seem as dangerous as the black panther her imagination had first suggested—uncaged, that blackness could only bring danger.

Her moment's unease soon vanished and she even found she could put on a front of quite passable nonchalance as now and then Harlem's hand brushed hers over the table. He was drinking vodka again, she noticed with misgivings, wondering if he realised how shocking she found it.

They all spilled out of the restaurant around three o'clock. 'Is this an especially long lunch or an everyday occurrence?' she asked Frank as she walked back to the car with him.

'I've known longer ones,' he informed her with a smile. 'But don't count on it happening every day. He knows when they need to unwind and when he has to crank them up. With Harlem everything has a purpose. He always has control.'

'So I'd guess.' She slid into the passenger seat. 'So I'd guess.'

CHAPTER FIVE

AS HARLEM had told her, Frank allotted her a drawing-board in his studio and for all day-to-day, practical purposes she worked from his studio. Only the project was her own for, of course, she was working on sets for Harlem's new company while Frank was busy with freelance commissions and his work for the National Ballet.

It was an ideal situation for Tiffany because it was inevitable she should pick up useful help in a busy studio like that. Frank himself was generous with his time and advice, and his two assistants made Tiffany welcome straight away and passed on anything she needed to know. People were coming in and out all the time, but after her second day, when she presented her ideas to Harlem as he had requested, he himself didn't come near the place and seemed content to trust her to get on with things without his interference.

She knew he was busy rehearsing next door. Frank's studio adjoined the theatre which, she learned, Harlem had rescued from developers who had been hoping to turn it into a night-club, some months before. 'It must have cost the earth!' she exclaimed when she heard this over coffee one morning in the studio as she took a break with Frank's assistants.

'He can buy the earth—should he be misguided enough to want it!' Jason, Frank's right-hand man, smiled. 'If Harlem were a normal, fun-loving individual, he'd retire now and live out his days in discreet riot in the South of France.'

'So why doesn't he?' she asked.

'Because he's a genius, or haven't you noticed? And geniuses never retire.'

'They don't even fade away,' added Gavin, the junior. 'At least, I can't see Harlem fading.'

'I thought geniuses burned themselves out?' suggested Tiffany lightly.

'He tried that, and nearly succeeded.'

'You mean his accident?'

Jason shrugged. 'That was the final fling.' He got up, and Tiffany saw his reluctance to say anything more as a mark of loyalty to Harlem. She was still the outsider. She didn't resent Jason's reticence, but it piqued her curiosity. Although Harlem had seemed to talk openly about what had happened to him she was aware that he had in fact said very little. Perhaps there wasn't much to say. Accidents happened. It was the aftermath and the way in which the victim coped or failed to cope in which the tragedy lay.

* * *

A week fled by. Tiffany took a morning off to say goodbye to everyone in college and already it seemed a lifetime ago that she had been a mere student, anxiously handing in projects and waiting to be graded. Now she was faced with the outside world, and the measure of her success would be marked up in a different way, first when she obtained Harlem's approval of her designs, then, more dramatically, when a paying audience and the critics were confronted with them. The opening date was only ten days ahead. She found it impossible to believe that Harlem had entrusted such a responsibility to her, but when she mentioned this to Frank he merely laughed.

'The only way to learn is to be thrown in at the deep end, love.'

She had to be content with that.

Pat lent her the book on positive thinking. She had been convinced it had worked for her ever since she had got the job she'd longed for. 'We'll all be working soon. It'll be strange to go on living in a student house. I expect we'll all be going our separate ways before long.' The three of them spent a nostalgic evening going over old times and promising to keep in touch when the inevitable happened.

Ginny wanted the latest on Harlem Barensky. 'There is no latest, Ginny,' Tiffany told her. 'I haven't seen him since that second morning when I showed him what I was going to do. I'm expecting a summons any day.' She bit her lip. 'I just hope he gets a move on. If he doesn't like what I've done, there's hardly going to be any time to change it.'

'He must trust you,' remarked Pat.

Tiffany frowned. 'Either that or it's a test of some sort. I remember what he said when we first talked. Everything's temporary. He meant my job, and I don't doubt he'll throw me out if I don't come up to scratch.' She spoke lightly, but her nerves were beginning to stretch to breaking point as days passed and there was no response from him.

'Frank,' she said next morning as soon as she got in, 'I've gone as far as I can with all this. It's reached the stage where I'm beginning to go round in circles. I really need to get Harlem's go-ahead so we can start work with the carpenters. Time seems horribly short.'

Frank raised his head from his drawing. 'Hasn't he been in touch?'

Tiffany shook her head.

'He was asking how you were getting on three or four days ago. I'm surprised you haven't heard anything. I'd get over there as soon as I could, if I were you.'

Tiffany was out of the door in two seconds. She hurried along the street and turned the corner of the block, running two at a time up the steps to the stage door. Surely Harlem hadn't been waiting for her to tell him she was ready? Days had been wasted if so. She hadn't slept properly until she felt the project was complete. Then there had been a long hiatus when she had had to fill out her time by putting the finishing touches to something she only guessed was on the right lines.

The doorman called out to her as she swept past, but she was in too much of a hurry to listen. She knew where Harlem would be.

She pushed open the door and walked in.

They were playing their tune—the one that came first in the sequence from which the rest of the show had sprung, and for a split second she was swept by a wave of something like regret that the closeness she had felt with him that first afternoon had remained undeveloped. Then a harsh voice cut into her thoughts.

'Who the hell is that? I thought I gave strict instructions nobody was to come in——'

Stepping round a corner of the flat, Tiffany found herself standing in the full glare of a battery of lights. The stage was drenched in it, picking out the stark forms of three dancers, their bodies, slim as whipcord, intertwined in an intricate tracery of limbs that broke apart as soon as Harlem's voice cut through the moment. Someone killed the music, and Harlem himself limped on to the stage, shielding his eyes with one hand.

'Miss Mulgrove, I do declare,' he announced

in tones of mock surprise. 'I'd given you up for dead at least.' She saw his lips snap shut. Then he swivelled without moving from the spot to include figures, as yet unseen, standing in the wings.

'Friends,' he declaimed with heavy irony, 'for those of you who haven't yet had the pleasure, meet our designer, Miss Tiffany Mulgrove. Yes, funds do indeed stretch so far, though some of you may have been puzzled as to why you'd seen no evidence of such extravagance. A bare stage, you might have thought. Why not? But I do assure you that was not my original intention, although circumstances have forced me to rethink the situation.' He paused, and Tiffany felt his eyes leap the intervening space and penetrate her own.

Holding his glance, she took a pace forward and opened her mouth. As if anticipating excuses, he held up a hand. 'This is such a special occasion for us all that I think it's time we took a break. Twenty minutes, everyone.' He banged his stick on the floor.

There was an off-stage confusion of activity, and then silence. The three dancers on stage vanished as lightly as sylphs.

'What the bloody hell have you been playing at? Can't you cope?' he demanded as soon as they were alone.

Tiffany swallowed hard, but forced herself to walk forward so she didn't have to shout.

'I finished days ago. I thought you were busy. I thought you would let me know when you wanted to see me,' she said as soon as she reached him.

'I don't believe this! Are you trying to tell me you've been cosily settled in Frank's studio, just sitting there—waiting to be summoned?'

'What else did you expect me to do?'

'What else?' he roared, brow furrowing. 'What the hell is this? Some kindergarten? It's work, my dear Miss Mulgrove. We have a show to do. We're a team. We pull together. We don't sit on our bottoms waiting for teacher to tell us what to do next!' He didn't move an inch towards her, but Tiffany knew that if he'd been able he would have reached forward and grabbed her by the scruff of the neck and given her a good shaking, so patent was his rage. She had never seen anyone express anger like this without moving a muscle. Every cell of his body seemed brittle with emotion. She began to shake. He seemed to annihilate her. She put up a hand.

'I came as soon as I knew I should,' she muttered weakly. 'Why didn't you tell me you expected me to come over?' *Now* she saw with hideous clarity how wrong she had been. She had no defence. *Why* had she been so stupid?

'You seem to be under the mistaken impression you're home and dry just because you've walked straight out of college into a job. But it's not the cosy number you obviously think. I guessed Frank was letting his heart rule his head when he suggested taking you on—you looked too fat when I first saw you, and I was right! Never trust a fat guy,' he said cruelly. 'Let *me* have lean and hungry men about me. The same with women. You're too comfortable, Tiffany, that's your trouble. Life doesn't owe you a living. You have to fight like a rat for scraps. And until you're hungry enough you'll never do it!'

'I don't know about all that,' she managed to say, running a hand nervously over her hips and wishing she could shrink to nothing. 'All I know is I finished the project several days ago. I thought——'

'I don't care a damn what you thought! You're not paid to think—like that,' he amended when he saw her lip curl. 'These dancers have been falling apart without a set. They need some idea what's on stage. Of course, they'll dance on water if you ask them——' He stopped. 'Where the hell is it, then?'

'The mock-up?'

'Of course, the mock-up. What do you imagine I mean, Santa Claus's fairy castle?'

'It's in the studio.'

'Then bring it over.' He enunciated the words as if she were feeble-minded.

Her earlier fears that it would all be hopelessly wrong swam to the surface. Did he expect her to bring over the models and all her drawings? 'Aren't you going to come over and see it for yourself?' she began.

'Are you serious?'

'All right.' She stumbled back, knocking against the flat behind her so that it shook wildly.

'Bloody hell, I can't take this!' Harlem swivelled with startling rapidity and disappeared into the wings. 'Tell her to get back within five minutes, otherwise she's out!' he yelled in a voice everyone could hear. An assistant materialised from nowhere.

'All right, I heard,' said Tiffany, tight-lipped, before he could say anything.

She flew out of the theatre and down the street, feeling that the hounds of hell were behind her. Why hadn't he made it clear he wanted her to come over? It was so unfair. And now she would have to show him her ideas when he was in the least likely mood to accept them. He was bound to find fault. God, God, she thought, why didn't I realise he wanted me to go over with them? How was I to know he expected *me* to make the first move?

She burst into the studio, oblivious of the startled glances of the two boys, and collected together the models she had made. Stacking them precariously on top of each other, she made her way gingerly towards the door.

'Want any help, sweetheart?' It was Gavin

'I've got to get these to Harlem within five

minutes, otherwise I'm out,' she told him, too distraught to put it any other way.

'No hassle. Keep still. I'll take the top one. OK?' Gavin seemed to think there was nothing unusual in her frantic haste, and he followed her out into the street with the flimsy model carefully tucked under one arm.

'Life always gets hysterical before an opening,' he told her as they hurried along. 'And Harlem's allowed a bit of temperament. Don't look so worried about it. Just stand up to him.'

'Might as well try standing up to a raging tornado,' she muttered. 'Anyway, thanks, Gavin.'

He pushed open the door on to the stage and helped her balance the model he had carried over on top of the others.

When he left she stepped on to the stage, expecting to find Harlem glowering at her centre stage, but the place was deserted.

She looked in vain for somewhere safe to place the models, but apart from the stage itself there wasn't anywhere and so she began to lower them gently to the floor. Only when she straightened did she realise that Harlem had been watching silently from the wings. Evidence of his presence came in the slow handclap as she stood up. Fuming, she waited to see what would happen next.

He stepped forward into the light. Dressed in a black T-shirt and tight black denims

which moulded themselves suggestively to
his muscular thighs, his long legs gave no
overt sign of his injury. But he stood there
without moving, looking her up and down,
like the baddie in a Western, she thought, all
lean masculinity, black as sin, thin and lethal
as a whip—High Noon.

'Congratulations,' he mocked. 'With your
record it's a miracle you didn't jettison the
whole lot on to the floor in a heap of broken
matchwood. I swear I didn't dare take a
breath till you'd finished.' He took a limping
step forward, and she noticed he was leaning
heavily on his stick as he moved. Then he
stopped, lifting it to point at one of the
models. 'Bring it here where I can see it. I
assume that's number one?'

Without speaking, Tiffany bent and then,
without looking at him either, carried the
model carefully across to him.

Harlem gave it a long, considering look.

After what seemed an age he simply
barked, 'Next!'

The old antagonism prickled up her body,
making her flesh tingle and her innards turn
to water. She dutifully placed the second
model at his feet.

'What's that?' He poked the end of his stick
into the model.

'It's the sheet of silk you said you wanted,'
she defended. She had used paper. It didn't
look at all like silk, but it fulfilled the

requirements of the model by taking up approximately the same amount of space to scale as the real thing.

'OK. Let's have the other one.'

A third time she went away, hating him, and dutifully laid her work at his feet.

There was an even longer silence, and at the end of it he said, 'We'll talk later. Their break's over now. Stay and watch. You can have a seat in the stalls if you can manage to climb down there without smashing the place up.'

Without looking at her, he turned away, banging three times with his stick on the wooden floor of the stage. At once it filled with dancers in gaudy practice gear. Marvelling at their discipline, she fled to the anonymity of the front stalls.

Did he like her work or not? she fumed. Was it a bad sign when he said he'd talk later? She tried to remember the particular inflections of his voice as he'd issued his terse commands, to glean some idea of his verdict, but all she could remember was the way his lips had tightened, the arch of his brow, the curve of his cheekbones, exotic, eloquent of his foreign heritage. The differences between them screamed in an agony that sent waves of frustration leaping through her body, and she suddenly knew that her absence from the theatre had been a deliberate attempt to keep him at a distance. She had been frightened

of coming face to face with him. It seemed
searingly obvious now. Her mind had played
a trick on her, deliberately blinding her to
the situation.

Coming face to face with him again, she
knew she was mad for him, just as Ginny
had jokingly said, all those days ago. To see
him again had been a blinding revelation, a
knife-in-the-gut experience—and the very
last thing she had ever expected. There had
been nothing like this in her entire life before
now. It was like stepping out of a cosy shell
into a blistering inferno.

The dancers went through their paces, and
though she tried to concentrate, to see how,
if at all, her feeble attempt to provide a set
for them might work, she could only see
Harlem, literally and figuratively, as he
leaned on his stick in the shadows in the
wings. His attention was concentrated
entirely on his dancers. She saw him
demonstrate a turn, a movement of an arm.
Each gesture was a pale shadow of what he
had formerly been capable of yet still
eloquent in a way that convinced her of his
greatness. She saw him change the angle of
a dancer's fingertips so that a whole sequence
was transformed, and she saw how readily
everyone responded, subtly aware of every
nuance of his command.

Convinced that these were her last hours
with him as part of his company, she tried to

imprint on her memory the little details of
his appearance that brought such a fever to
her soul. She wanted to remember everything
about him.

She had failed him, she thought miserably,
that was all that could be said. His anger was
justified. His disappointment in her was
obvious. He said he wanted one hundred per
cent success. Well, she had given everything.
And it wasn't enough.

She heard him bring the rehearsal to an
end. Everyone was dismissed, and eventually
he stood for a moment on the empty stage,
exhaustion lining his face. Then he was
shading his eyes with his hands, peering out
into the darkness of the stalls.

'Miss Mulgrove? Are you still with us?'

She made a sound, but doubted whether
he heard it.

'If you would be so kind as to step up,' he
called.

'Just coming,' she managed to croak,
hurrying to the steps to the pit and
scrambling up on to the stage.

He watched her come towards him with an
ironic twist to his mouth. 'You flatter our
workshop staff, my dear. Let's hope they can
live up to your high expectations,' he said as
she came within speaking distance.

'Sorry?'

'I don't mind paying overtime, but if, as you
claim, this was ready several days ago I do

think you might have let us all in on it so
they could be given their instructions and
have organised their work without making
extra claims on our resources. However, I'm
sure the result will be well worth it.'

'Sorry?' said Tiffany again.

'What's the matter?'

'I don't understand,' she blurted.

'Russian any better?' He broke into a
stream of incomprehensible syllables that
were at once savage and caressing, his eyes
sweeping her flushed face with malicious
amusement. He broke off, and added softly,
'Don't imagine I'm backing down on what I
said earlier. You've led an unimaginably
comfortable life so far. But if you're really
going to achieve your full potential we must
do something to break the spell that has you
in its grip. Right?'

She could only stare at him. There was too
much to take in.

'Let's go down to the workshop,' he said
abruptly. 'You're not saying much to me.
Perhaps you'll be more articulate with the
carpenters?'

'You mean you accept what I've put
together?' she asked hesitantly.

'I think it's rather clever. Frank may well
be proved right.' He held out an arm. 'Please?
Would you?'

In a daze Tiffany took his arm, unsure
whether he was leaning on her, or whether it

was she who was leaning on him. All she could think was that a miracle had happened. He liked her work! Harlem Barensky had given her his approval!She felt she could be his slave for ever more. He could say whatever cruel things he liked about her figure. She had no choice but to follow him faithfully for as long as he desired!

After they left the workshop he turned to her at the bottom of the stairs leading up to his apartment. 'I take back what I said,' he admitted generously. 'You handled all their queries with great dexterity. So, now, what are you doing for lunch?'

'I've got sandwiches——' she began, still reeling from his unexpected praise.

'Forget those. Come up and join me?'

'Thank you.' She went on ahead, pausing at the top as he came up beside her. As he stepped on to the landing she was overwhelmed by his lethal length only inches away. The same magic as before seemed to draw her towards him, and this time he was aware of it almost before she was herself. Then his arms reached out for her, and she knew there would be no reprieve by telephone, no Frank Shore to interrupt.

'Tiffany.' He leaned across her to open the door, pulling her roughly into his arms as he did so. 'That's better, that's so much better, my love.' His dark head rested against the

side of her neck and his arms came right
round her, lifting her slightly off her feet and
massaging her whole body in the sudden
heat of his embrace. He lifted his head with
a little laugh. 'Tell me, Tiffany, were you
deliberately avoiding me?' His hands snaked
over her shoulders and gripped her face
between his two hands so he could gaze
down into her eyes.

She tried to blink away, but he held her in
a firm grip. 'I believe you were, weren't you?'

'Yes,' she admitted at last. 'I think I must
have been without realising it.'

He knew why. Her admission betrayed the
truth, but he seemed to have expected it, for her
words were the sign he seemed to need to take
her into his arms, moulding her softness to his
hard frame, lowering his lips carefully on to
her own in a merging of sweet fires that brought
a sound of soft surrender to her throat. His
hands splayed over her shoulders, bringing her
more urgently against him, and she felt her
mouth yield to the growing need that seemed
to sweep over him.

With a small twist of her head she forced
herself out of his arms and stepped back.
'Don't, Harlem.'

'Frightened?'

'I don't know you.'

'That's the object of the exercise, isn't it?
To get to know each other?' he murmured
throatily.

'Don't, I—that's not the sort of knowing I mean.' As he moved forward again, pinning her against the wall at the top of the stairs, she ran her hands down over her hips, flinching back as he started to lower his head again. 'You can't want to kiss me, you say such horrible things—you think I'm fat—I'm not your type——'

'Hell, is that what's bothering you?' He laughed huskily against the side of her face, hugging her in his arms and rocking her back and forth. 'You're not fat, you silly idiot, only a little overweight compared to my anorexic dancers.'

'But just now you said I was.'

'I meant figuratively. You know that speech from *Julius Caesar,* don't you? I meant I'm not like Caesar—I *want* people around me who are lean with ambition.' His lips traced a tantalising path down the line of her nose, ending with a little kiss on her pouting lips. 'And it's true you've had a comfortable life. I can read it in your face.' He pushed her towards the door of his suite. 'Let's go inside.'

With a feeling that she ought to resist him Tiffany allowed him to usher her over the threshold into the corridor of green tiles. Then with a feeling that control was slipping away she felt his arm drape over her shoulders, and together they began to make their way towards one of the closed doors that lay ahead.

CHAPTER SIX

HARLEM pushed open a door at the far end of the corridor with his stick, and as it swung open he called, 'Hey! *Bábushka!*'

He went on inside, and Tiffany heard an excited voice saying something she couldn't understand before she followed him. By the time she went in he had, despite his disability, swept the occupant of the kitchen into his arms and was hugging her back and forth, ignoring her struggles to be put down. Grinning, he replaced her gently on the floor.

Tiffany confronted a person who looked like a miniature version of everybody's granny. She alternately wiped tears of laughter from her button eyes and scraped her wispy grey hair back into its bun as she nodded a greeting to Tiffany.

'Treasure of my heart,' Harlem smiled, 'and speaks not a word of English.' He hugged the old lady again, dwarfing her with his bulk, adding, 'But as well as Russian she's fortunate enough to speak the international language of cuisine, as you'll shortly discover.' He said something to her that Tiffany couldn't follow, and she turned back to the oven from which she had evidently just been about to lift a cooking pot.

Tiffany felt swamped by mixed feelings. Desire to feel a continuation of Harlem's tantalising touch raged through her. At the same time, however, she felt weak with relief that the crunch hadn't come yet. She knew she couldn't lightly cast her principles to the wind and follow wherever Harlem's hot passions seemed to be leading, but at the same time she couldn't see how she could summon the will-power to resist. One touch and she melted.

She smiled with relief at the apple-cheeked *Bábushka*, and prayed that her presence was permanent.

Now Harlem's eyes were sweeping over her flushed face. 'A little glass of vodka, some bortsch and caviare—and time to unwind perhaps and get to know each other, yes?' His eyes silvered when he saw her expression. 'With a chaperon in the kitchen, Miss Mulgrove, what more could you desire?'

She heard herself try to give a smooth laugh, but it sounded too shaky to convince anyone that she was still in the driver's seat, and with Harlem giving her a penetrating glance that seemed to strip her to the soul she knew she was fooling no one.

'Come!' He moved on ahead, leaning on his stick, but progressing rapidly so that she had to hurry to keep up.

When he pushed open the door to the sitting-room he nodded towards the drinks cabinet. 'Sorry I have to ask you to wait on me.' He threw himself down on the leather chesterfield and closed his eyes. 'Hell, I'm exhausted and it's all systems go till the opening. I was making mental plans to get by without a set when you didn't show up. I thought I'd let Frank talk me into making a real hash of things. I'm sorry, Tiffany,' he said, opening his eyes when he felt her come close, 'I had my doubts about you. I guess I was wrong and Frank was right.'

She wondered if he meant he'd been wrong in every respect, but didn't feel confident enough to ask.

He took the drink she offered and threw it back, and she stood for a minute looking down at him and wondering if she would be stepping out of line to say something about that at least.

'What is it?' He read her mind. 'I do watch it, you know. It's not getting out of hand and it's not always necessary.' He looked at his empty glass. 'That's the last one until this evening, all right?'

'I don't know much about the pressures you're under,' she admitted, sitting gingerly on the edge of the sofa next to him. 'I've no right to judge you, but——'

'No one's keener on staying in good physical shape than me, sweetheart, don't worry. Your concern is touching.' He reached for her hand. 'Thank you.' He drew his lips back in that sudden brilliant smile that had stormed her defences already, and said, 'So now, what about you?'

'What about me?' she laughed nervously, eyeing the door and straining to hear providential sounds of help from the kitchen.

'I know precious little about you.'

'There's nothing much to know,' she told him candidly. 'You seem to have me neatly packaged already.'

'Oh, come, now, don't be so modest. There are a million things I don't know. What about your family? Brothers? Sisters?'

'No brothers,' she replied, pleased for the reprieve of neutral ground. Then she told him about her younger sister Fay, a law student in Manchester, the family home in Fareham, the childhood pony, the holidays in Lyme Regis and later Tuscany, and the comprehensive school where she had always come top in art.

Then she told him about coming up to college, about the house shared with a group of other students, about Ginny who was a fan of his, and Pat who designed furniture. 'You really were right,' she concluded just as lunch was brought through. 'I've led a boringly uneventful life and you were right when you accused me of being cosy, too.'

'Never mind,' he observed sardonically. 'Life has a knack of taking a helping hand in that direction. Make the most of it while you've got it. One simple mistake and you might find the whole cosy lot wiped out forever. God save it never happens.' He turned abruptly and said something in Russian to the *Bábushka*, and Tiffany was painfully aware of the differences between them. It made her yearn to know him, to penetrate his mystery and dissolve the miles of culture and experience that separated them—until their souls touched as knowingly as did their bodies.

Under the lively silver and black gaze of his eyes she could only pick at her food, and he observed her with some amusement when she refused second helpings. 'I really wasn't referring to your figure when I said you were fat, you know. I think you have a magnificent body—from what I've seen of it under all those baggy smocks you wear.' He grinned as she blushed. 'What happened to that wicked black leather outfit? I was rather hoping I'd be seeing that again. Will you wear it tonight if I promise to take you to a club?'

She gulped. 'Me?' She imagined all the famous women she had seen him with in the pages of the Press.

'You're a funny mixture, Tiffany. I'm thirty-three. I guess the age difference is too big?' He raised an eyebrow. 'You have the body of a mature woman, and it makes me forget how young you really are.'

'Twenty-one isn't young.'

'Not if you have a thirst for fame before you're twenty-five,' he laughed.

'How did you know——' she burst out, then broke off with embarrassment.

He laughed softly. 'Trick question. If you'd denied it I'd have been disappointed beyond belief.'

'I told my flat-mate Ginny that working for you would be like walking through a minefield,' she began, then blushed when she remembered what she had meant then. 'And it is, in lots of ways,' she added lamely.

'I expect you'll make it through to the other side,' he observed. 'Now, how about coffee and a stroll on the roof?'

'Shall I ask *Bábushka*?' She rose when he did.

'Her name's Anya. *Bábushka* means little granny—it's a term of endearment.'

'I'm sorry.'

'No need. Tell her where we'll be. I'm sure you can mime it with those enormous violet eyes!' He moved awkwardly from his chair, waving her away when she made as if to come and help him. Biting her lip, she left him to it, and popped her head around the kitchen door to manage somehow to convey her thanks for a scrumptious meal and hand on the message about coffee, too. Anya's sharp eyes were full of friendliness and she nodded her understanding.

Harlem was outside, and she had to trace

him through a maze of jungle plants under the glass roof before stepping out to find him leaning against a brick chimney-stack, gazing out across the City towards the river.

'It's marvellous up here!' she exclaimed as she stepped up beside him.

'When one door closes another one opens,' he said enigmatically, going on to explain briefly that, without the final curtain on his career as a dancer with leading companies around the world, it would never have crossed his mind to settle down in one place.

'This theatre's coming on the market at the right time was like a gift from heaven. And after what heaven had just done to me I guess it was a sort of apology.' He looked up with a quizzical expression as if expecting a flash of lightning in response; then, without waiting, he took her hand and in almost the same tone said, 'I want to kiss those lips properly. I'm going to kiss them, damn it.'

His fingers began to slide up her right arm inside the baggy woollen jumper she was wearing. 'I've wanted to hold you in my arms for so long. It seems like a small lifetime,' he murmured as his experienced hands drew an immediate spasm of pleasure from her. 'Your face is perfection and your breasts pure heaven.' He lowered his face to press it in the V of her neckline, pulling her up into his arms so that her back arched and she pressed helplessly against him. 'You've no idea how sick I get of looking at flat-chested girls who could be boys. It's paradise to hold a real woman.'

Shivering from head to foot, Tiffany swallowed hard. 'I expect there are plenty of those around for a man like you.'

'Lucky me,' he replied with an ironic inflection. His lips pressed softly against the pale skin at her throat, trailing down and back in a teasing pattern that just avoided the softest skin below the loose neck of her lavender sweater so that she couldn't help arching herself even further to push her breasts closer still to the tantalising touch that just skimmed them. With a little shiver she felt his expert hands ride up inside her sweater, loosening her silk camisole at the waist and slithering inside it, over her burning skin. Then his fingers began to cup and curve around her naked breasts, teasing the hardening nipples till she wanted to swoon with pleasure. Nothing in her imagination had prepared her for the magic he was weaving. It cast a bewitchment over her senses that made everything else fade.

'Wait, my honey, Anya is coming out.' Regretfully he drew down her sweater and rested both hands on her shoulders, and he was standing looking down at her like this as Anya appeared round the corner bearing a tray. With a rapid burst of Russian she said something to Harlem, following it up with a wicked laugh, and even though Tiffany hadn't been able to follow the words she guessed it was some ribald comment about the two of them. She bit her lip.

'Take no notice. She has a peasant sense of humour.' He called something after her, and as soon as she was out of sight brought his lips down with careful deliberation against Tiffany's own. It was a kiss like slow fire, igniting a fuse along her veins that grew and grew and finally burst in an explosion that swept through her like a fire-storm.

'Tiffany, baby, hold on . . .' he groaned, lifting his head a fraction and gazing with bleared eyes into her own. She felt her lashes droop and everything became hazy, a small sound of surrender escaping her throat at the same moment. In a daze she felt him scoop her up against his power-packed muscles, running ravaging kisses over her face and neck, his hands searching beneath a tangle of wool and silk for the throbbing peaks she was shamelessly offering to his touch. Then, with a groan, she felt him fasten her pulsating body hard against his own, stilling it with the force of a will that seemed superhuman until their two hearts slowed and steadied, only the undulations of frustrated passion betraying the effort it had cost him to call a halt.

'I'm sorry——' She tried to break away, shamefaced at allowing herself to be taken over by this demon he had unleashed, but her body refused to relinquish its hold on his as if fixed by an unseen force.

'Not as sorry as I am,' he murmured, stroking her dark hair from her nape, 'but probably for a different reason.' She felt his lips move against her hair in small consoling kisses. When he looked at her he gave a small grimace.

'This wasn't planned, Tiffany. At least—I imagined I might be unable to resist kissing those pouting lips of yours. But this . . .' He appeared consciously to release the tension that still throbbed through his frame. 'This is unplanned.'

He very slowly released her and moved a few steps away, sitting down on a brick ledge near the edge of the roof, his stick between his legs. 'I think we'd better cool it, don't you?' His eyes were two dark pools drawing her in.

'Cool?' She felt anything but cool. Her world was a confusion of flame. Even though he had now released her she could feel his touch lick her body in every part.

His lips set in a straight line. 'Hell, we have to work together. I value that more than I value any sexual escapade. They're there for the asking,' he judged brutally. 'What you can offer the company as a designer is worth too much to risk for a bit of sex.'

She shuddered as if whipped. Her hands scraped along the brick wall behind her, and she steadied herself but couldn't bring herself to say anything in reply.

'That's settled, then. I'm glad you agree. You're too sensible and too ambitious not to.' He got up abruptly, turning so she couldn't read his face. 'Drink your coffee. I've got the afternoon rehearsal in fifteen minutes. You may as well sit in on it for an hour before you disappear into the workshops.' He swung back. 'Forget this, Tiffany. I'm sorry it happened. Do you take sugar?'

'What?' Her eyes widened. She drew in a shuddering breath before nodding speechlessly. She was still pressing against the brick stack for support when he sugared her coffee, stirred it and held it out to her. Forcing herself to behave normally, she moved forward to take it, avoiding his glance, thoughts frozen wordlessly in her head. He seemed in control, talking of this and that as if nothing out of the ordinary had happened between them. She nodded and shook her head, and made one or two comments that seemed to pass for ordinary conversation without drawing from him any indication that she was failing to make sense. She was on automatic pilot but he didn't seem to notice.

They went down to the theatre shortly afterwards, and all she could think was that there now seemed to be a good eighteen inches between them as they made their way across the stage. In her previous place in the front row of the stalls she underwent a peculiar form of torture, having to watch him with the glare of the stage lights illuminating every last, tantalising detail of his appearance.

Later she had to go to the workshops to supervise the construction of the set, and it was after six by the time she wearily returned backstage to pick up her things. Frank's warning that Harlem was always in control, that he knew when to wind up the clockwork figures in his theatre, and when to wind them down again, had drummed through her brain all afternoon.

Harlem was chatting to a couple of dancers in the corridor and, when she drew level, he put out a hand. 'Don't go just yet. We have some arrangements to make, yes?'

'Do we?'

He shook his head reprovingly. 'Short memory, Miss Mulgrove.' Their conversation at an end, the dancers went out and Harlem turned to her with a weary smile. 'Tonight's still on, as far as I'm concerned.'

'Tonight?' Her brow puckered, then she recalled his invitation and the bargain that had accompanied it. 'Do you think it's a good idea in the circumstances?' she asked, her feelings running wild at the thought of an evening together.

'Nothing's going to happen in public,

honey. I'll bring the crew along to make sure.'

She nodded. 'Same requirements?' she asked, cool violet eyes sweeping his face as if she were really in control.

'Wonderful! Make it really tough for me.' He turned with a smoky laugh, then swung back again. 'I've just remembered, I don't know where you live.'

'It's all right,' she said hurriedly. 'I'll get a taxi.' She couldn't bear the thought of his penetrating her private retreat when it was the only place outside his control she had left.

He looked uncertain, but her expression must have convinced him it was useless to argue. 'Be here around nine, then. Frank and Marguerite are having dinner with me to discuss finance at seven so there'll be no possibility of anything——' he hesitated, adding abruptly—'of anything happening by accident.'

His prediction was quite correct and, accompanied by three or four members of the company as well as Frank and Marguerite, they formed quite an entourage as they swept into a Mayfair club around ten o'clock that night.

Harlem was obviously a special customer, and there were several tables already reserved for them, buckets of champagne glittering under the disco lights, as they went in. Straight away the dancers hit the floor as if they hadn't spent the whole day slaving at rehearsals, and Tiffany watched enviously as they drew all eyes.

'Better than the usual floor show. I reckon they ought to pay them,' commented Harlem, his face blank as he watched them gyrate under the lights. 'Time was——' He broke off. 'Hey, let's relax! We'll make out together in a while if you can bear to carry me once around the floor!'

'You sound very American sometimes, Harlem,' she commented, her heart wrenching with compassion as she realised what an effort it cost him to be sitting down when he would rather be on the floor, at one with the music like everyone else.

'Not surprising, really. My mother's American. A six-foot-two-inch Texan, to be exact.' He laughed at her surprise. 'Didn't you wonder how I got the name Harlem?'

She nodded. 'I thought maybe it was a stage name or something.'

'No way.'

'Tell me about her,' she suggested, trying to conjure up this new image he had presented her with.

'She was a night-club singer in her heyday. Harlem meant vitality, inspiration, to her. She met my father when he was on tour with the Bolshoi. Their liaison caused something of an international incident, apparently. I was born in the States and spent the first three years of my life there. Then I was shipped back to Russia for my education. That's where I learned to dance. My father wanted that.'

'Would you have chosen to be a dancer yourself?'

He smiled. 'I guess it's in the blood. My Georgian ancestors are great dancers.'

'So where do you think of as home?' she asked, wondering how she could understand him.

'Home? I thought home is where the heart is? Or is that too much of a cliché for the original Miss Mulgrove?'

'I'm coming round to clichés,' she confessed. 'My life seems to be running from one to another at the moment.' She blushed.

'You're talking about this lunchtime?' he asked sharply.

She nodded

'I'm sorry, Tiffany.' He reached for her hand across the table. 'It'd be crazy to jeopardise a good working relationship for—what? Something that at best can only be a passing fancy.'

'For you, you mean?'

He seemed to take an age to reply, and when he did his tone was sombre. 'Not only for me. For you too. You are so very young, you know. Your needs are changing all the time. You are only now beginning to form yourself into the person you will eventually become. I couldn't expect you to want to tie yourself down to a has-been like myself.' He laughed. It was a harsh sound. Despite his show of humour she once again glimpsed the stratum of bitterness within his soul.

'Harlem,' she whispered, her heart torn with pain for him, 'I can't let you think that.'

'What?'

'You're not a has-been, and never will be. Heavens, if that's true, what chance has everybody else?'

'Maybe they are never-beens and never-will-bes.' He laughed acidly and as a waiter skimmed by he put out a hand. 'More champagne, *tovarich*, why so slow tonight?' He leaned back in his chair and called to the others. 'Lana! Maurice! Why is nobody drinking? Such straight faces! Come on, my friends! We are on the verge of a great new venture! Let's drink to the glittering future that lies in wait!'

If Tiffany hadn't heard his earlier words she wouldn't have been aware of the irony in what he was saying or have noticed the sudden twist of that mobile mouth as he uttered such sentiments, and, as the champagne corks popped and everyone laughingly raised their glasses, it seemed as if she was the only one to be aware of the note of desperation in his voice.

CHAPTER SEVEN

IF THE dancers behaved like disciplined militia during rehearsals, in real life their behaviour was quite different. Svetlana, in particular, the thin-as-a-whip leading dancer, took liberties with Harlem in public which would have made Tiffany blush to contemplate in private. Only his comment about flat-chested girls made her wonder if perhaps she was wasting her time. To her chagrin, however, Harlem appeared to have forgotten what he'd said and seemed to enjoy the whole performance, fielding the whispered endearments in Russian with a wicked glint in his eyes that left Tiffany in no doubt of their gist. She watched, while pretending not to, as the blonde persuaded him on to the dance floor where she proceeded to twine around his scarcely moving frame in a way that should have got them both thrown out. Tiffany herself hadn't had an opportunity to dance with him before he had been claimed, and she felt a heady mixture of relief and disappointment.

Frank pulled her to her feet. 'We designers should stick together. It's denting to the ego to be on a dance floor with this crowd. I'm glad you're here as moral support.' A few minutes later he gave her an approving glance. 'I guess I spoke too soon. You're a real little mover, Tiffany.'

She smiled, almost enjoying herself, and couldn't help saying, 'Not a bad-looking kid, eh?' And to his startled glance she added, 'I did an awful thing that day I came to the interview. Quite by accident I overheard you and Harlem arguing about me. I've felt guilty about it ever since. I hope you don't mind my mentioning it?'

Frank laughed uproariously, slipping his arms around her hips and swaying with her to the music as he asked her how it happened. She told him how surprised she'd been to find Harlem had changed his mind about her.

'I'd earmarked a couple of others for the short list, and we saw them that morning,' he explained. 'I'd saved you to last because I felt you were the one, but I wanted Harlem to see the others so he could put you in context. It was a gut feeling when I saw your work. I knew you were special, and I knew he could tell, too. I don't know what made him pretend to have doubts.'

She felt his hands slide over the soft leather trousers, moulding her hips sensuously between them. She pretended to dance a few steps to put a safer distance between them, and he let her go, his grey eyes conveying the fact that he'd got the message. Then he said,

'Harlem's a free spirit, Tiffany. He has no need to tie himself down to anyone. Don't hurt yourself.'

Her face drained of colour. 'Am I so transparent?' she quivered, her defences in disarray for a moment.

'You're all right. It's the trial by fire all females go through when they come near him.' He reached out for her, a friendly hand on her waist. 'I've got a sympathetic way with broken hearts. Remember that.'

The incident was over. For the rest of the evening Tiffany tried not to glance in Harlem's direction too often. It was when she was beginning to assume she was safe that he reached out for her, oblivious to Lana's derisory glance as he insisted she come on to the floor with him.

'I can't dance,' she warned, self-consciously aware of critical eyes following her.

'Makes two of us,' he quipped, pulling her into his arms.

'You seemed to be doing quite well just now,' she came back in a choky voice, as her senses were suddenly engulfed in the raw male presence of him.

'Call that dancing?' He killed the bitterness that sprang instantly into his eyes, and instead slid his hands suggestively over her rear in its second skin of leather. 'I suspected you might play safe and turn up in one of your woolly sweaters,' he murmured in her ear. 'I like a girl who can't resist playing with fire. I only hope you can handle it!'

'You promised I'd be safe,' she answered, trying to keep herself erect and not melt into his arms as all her senses demanded. 'Surely you keep promises, Mr Barensky?'

'I do indeed, Miss Mulgrove. Watch this space!'

Not sure what he meant, she was relieved when he stopped talking and let her concentrate on the music. With a lot of self-control she could just cope with feeling his body close to hers, but she couldn't cope with his husky voice and the outrageous things he seemed to be hinting in her ear at the same time. Somehow or other she endeavoured to survive through it. Not until the early hours was a move made to break up the party.

A shared taxi dropped her off first and, without further harm, she watched it from the porch as it disappeared into the night bearing, among others, Harlem . . . and Lana.

Tiffany expected that in the hectic days that preceded the opening her mind would be so fully occupied with getting the set right that she wouldn't have time for moony speculations about Harlem's love life. But the opposite seemed to be the case. He was there all the time. In her mind and in her sight. In her thoughts and, like a dark marauder, in her secret dreams at night.

She re-read Pat's book on positive think-ing, and thought of taking up meditation. She considered aversion therapy. She had supper once or twice with Frank, and went to a party or two with Rafe and some of the gang from college. But none of it seemed to work. The next morning she would be back to square one the minute she set eyes on Harlem. He, in his turn, seemed to have forgotten he had ever pirated kisses from her willing lips, and instead treated her like a cog in a smooth-running machine that needed his occasional mechanical supervision.

'It's working well!' he exclaimed, when he happened to turn to find her standing next to him in the wings the day before the technical run-through. 'That silk sheet is a stroke of sheer genius.'

'That was your idea,' she reminded.

'Was it?' He looked puzzled. 'Anyway, you managed to jigsaw the whole thing together.' He seemed preoccupied and she moved away. It was the closest to a conversation they had had for nearly a week. It wasn't so much winter between them as that dead time of year between winter and spring when nothing seemed to be happening. With them nothing *was* happening, she reminded herself, nor was there any promise of springtime ahead. Remembering what Frank had told her, she felt she should offer prayers of gratitude.

On the morning of the technical rehearsal
Tiffany was sitting in the stalls in her usual
place when Frank joined her, and just before
the lights came up Jason and Gavin slipped
into the row behind them. Tiffany felt
voiceless with nerves, wondering just what
the three professionals would think. Then
Harlem appeared through the swing doors at
the side. Oh, God, she thought as her heart
gave a lurch, he's coming to sit next to us.
She gripped the arm-rests of her seat when
his familiar shape came towards them as the
house lights went down. It was pitch-dark by
the time he slid into the seat next to hers, but
her antennae picked up the subtle presence
of him, confirmation of his proximity coming
from the masculine fragrance that drifted her
way.

I'll never be able to concentrate, she
thought, trying not to turn her head. Stiffly
she remained eyes front as the lights came
up on a stage empty but for her own design.

'Sensational, darling!' It was Frank. He
gripped her hand where it lay on her lap, then
went on holding it as the dancers made their
appearance. Tiffany wanted to get her hand
back but couldn't. Frank seemed to have
forgotten he was holding it. She felt Harlem
shift in his seat.

Later Jason and Gavin were fulsome in

their praise. 'I'm quite green-eyed,' announced Jason in everyone's hearing. 'I wish I were twenty-one and not over the hill at thirty!' He kissed her on both cheeks. 'All that heartache for nothing!' He knew how worried she had been from the start.

'Heartache?' It was Lana. 'Never mind, sugar plum.' She gave Tiffany a friendly pat on the shoulder. 'You have a wonderful career ahead of you.'

Jason gave Tiffany an odd look when she'd gone. 'Oops, have I missed something?'

Tiffany shook her head. 'Haven't a clue what she's on about, Jay.'

'She's spot on about the career, anyway.' He patted her arm. 'Frank deserves a big kiss.'

Tiffany turned away. She'd liked Frank from the first, but the thought of having to kiss any other lips than Harlem's was like a knife-wound.

Everyone wanted to leave quickly to unwind after Harlem had gone through a few notes with them, and Tiffany was pulling on her wool coat to go home when he came over to her. 'Hang on a minute, darling,' he said in an abstracted tone. 'I want to make a slight change.' He said one or two goodbyes, then turned back to her.

'It's working well and everybody seems happy with it. But I wonder if we could move the hoop to give Maurice a bit more room after he makes that entrance of his?'

The entrance he was referring to was a spectacular one, involving a hoop and a series of Maurice's famous leaps. 'I'd hate him to break his neck in the first five minutes,' he added.

'I'd hate him to break his neck anyway!'

He gave a quick, flashing smile. 'I'll take the responsibility if he does. You've done a nice safe job here. Look,' he moved away, beckoning her to follow, 'this is what I mean.' He moved painfully over to the hoop, and for a moment they discussed the technicalities of repositioning it.

When they finished he turned to her with a small frown. 'What was that about heartache I overheard just now?'

'I don't know.' She pretended to look puzzled.

'Don't lie to me. Are there rumours?'

'What about?' she asked, avoiding his glance.

'You know damned well what about.'

'I'm sorry, I haven't a clue. Do you mean about you and Lana?' she asked sweetly.

'Damn Lana, I'm not talking about her and you know it.'

'Then maybe you should be. If there are any rumours going the rounds they certainly won't involve *us*. You hardly acknowledge my existence!' She spoke more vehemently than she'd intended, and automatically put a hand to her mouth, knowing she had almost given herself away.

'I told you I can't afford to let anything happen between us, Tiffany.'

'Do I care?' she demanded, her voice rising. 'You surely don't imagine you're the only man in my life, do you? With the universe full of men?' She gave a hard laugh.

'They're always kissing you, too, I suppose?'

'What if they are?' She glared at him, her face white, and asked fiercely, 'Why shouldn't other men kiss me?'

'Like Frank, for instance?'

'So what?'

'I saw him holding your hand in the run-through. How long has that been going on?'

'Mind your own damned business, Mr Barensky!' she ground out, getting her voice under control though her heart was beginning to thud with the effort.

'I need to know what's happening in my company,' he snapped.

'Need? Why? Just so you can satisfy your sneaking curiosity? You're like some petty dictator!' she flared. 'Trying to keep tabs on us all! What the hell has our private life to do with you?'

'I'm not interested in keeping tabs on everybody, only on you, and of course it's something to do with me—what you do, who you——'

'Yes?' she stabbed.

'Who you go to bed with,' he concluded in a lowered voice, turning at the same time and limping over to the wings as if to cut off her reply.

'Has it? Has it indeed?' she shouted after him, angered by the way he seemed to think he owned her though he never did anything about it. 'Tough luck, Mr dog-in-the-manger Barensky. Because you'll never know, will you?'

He swung back at this taunt, his face as black as thunder. 'Won't I, by God? Won't I just?' With an effort he came back to where she stood and she saw with distress the way he was leaning heavily on his stick, his eyes turning dark with pain. 'Come here, you bitch,' he ground out.

'How dare you call me a bitch?' She was suddenly beside herself. All the pent-up frustration of the past few days, the pre-first-night nerves, the agony of knowing he would never be hers, came raging to the surface to swamp the tenderness she really felt. She took a step forward, for the space of a heartbeat convinced she was going to raise her hand to strike him.

Then shame overtook her, flooding her face with crimson, and instead she choked, 'I can't stand men like you, Harlem Barensky. You're full of conceit. So sure any woman who crosses your path is going to fall for you. You're dead inside, Harlem. There's nothing but a big zero where your heart should be.

Now get away! Get out of my life! I hate the sight of you!' She felt tears of impotent rage scald her cheeks in a rapid flood and, dashing her hand across her face, she gave him one last flashing glance before turning and walking rapidly from the stage.

Next morning came the dress rehearsal, and after that the company were to have the afternoon off to hype themselves up for the première that evening. The atmosphere was electric when Tiffany arrived backstage at ten o'clock after a sleepless night. Prepared for a confrontation with Harlem at some point during the morning, she was determined to freeze him out, but he was busy backstage and didn't come out front to watch at all. She noticed that the change he had suggested worked well, and Maurice gave her a thumbs up, earning a reprimand from the wings, as he walked off.

Feeling that her job was done, she left as soon as the final piece began, taking a Tube to Covent Garden to get as far away from Harlem as she could. The weather was sultry, and by the look of the dusty streets she realised they must be in the middle of one of those unexpected heatwaves that sometimes occurred in early July. Such had been her involvement with Harlem and the show that she hadn't even noticed.

With her jacket over one arm she wandered

aimlessly about among the bright stalls of crafted goods, scarcely aware of her surroundings, though her glance automatically glossed over pretty hand-painted mirrors, intricate embroideries, gaudy toys, frail shells and trinkets of all kinds.

Why had she said those things to Harlem yesterday? Did she really feel he had no heart? She supposed she did. The question had pounded through her head all night, bringing a resolution no nearer.

Recalling the many times she had seen that bedrock of bitterness beneath the controlled expressions he allowed to pass across his face, she could only put it down to the pain of wounded vanity. He had been an astonishing success, almost at the summit of his achievements, and her heart cracked with sorrow at how he must feel to have had it all snatched away by fate. Yet he had managed to establish himself in another way and again his fame was out of the ordinary. What more could he want? Surely it was nothing but overweening pride that made him feel so bitter now?

It was as if nothing mattered except his pride, his wounded ego. He didn't seem to realise that he was once again at the top of the tree. Tonight's performance would be living proof. But she guessed it wouldn't change him.

A part of her knew she could never fully

appreciate what it must be like to be one of the world's greatest dancers and then to be suddenly crippled, scarcely able to shuffle round the floor of a disco. But many people suffered more and managed to survive—and still have heart enough to care for others, too.

Her excursion to Covent Garden had had a purpose other than to take her mind off Harlem, and she came away from one of the boutiques with a dress that would see her through the première. There would be a backstage party afterwards.

'Sweets for the kids,' Frank had announced. 'Then we all sit around, biting our nails for the notices in the early editions. Damn the critics!'

'You won't say that when they start throwing roses,' Jason had commented with a smile.

Harlem doesn't realise how lucky he is to have all these people rooting for him, Tiffany had observed in silent condemnation.

It was a figured chiffon outfit, with harem pants and a plunging top to make the most of her assets, that finally caught her eye. She didn't care that it was verging on the indecent. It was an act of defiance to slither into it that evening as if she had to rub in what he had thrown away.

Ginny, Pat and a whole crowd from college were treating the event like a fancy-dress show, and were coming backstage to the

party, too. If they'd been reluctant she would
have twisted their arms. There was no way
she was going to face the evening by herself.
If she played it right she need never talk to
Harlem Barensky again. And once the show
was well and truly on the road she would
hand in her notice, or whatever one did in
Harlem's employment. She couldn't imagine
it had ever happened before. But there was a
first time for everything.

She avoided going backstage beforehand,
for Frank had warned her that the
atmosphere would be like a keg of dynamite
with first-night nerves, but instead she let
herself drift with the others to the stalls.
There wasn't an empty seat in the house by
the time the lights dimmed. Tiffany held her
breath. Then the music began to play.

CHAPTER EIGHT

THE applause was a rainstorm, hundreds of small separate sounds swelling to one single endless cloudburst. Tiffany joined in, applauding the dancers, applauding the musicians, and applauding most of all the brilliance of Harlem's invention, prouder than she had ever expected that she was part of a company which was clearly destined to hit the heights. Someone at the back started calling for Harlem by name, and the rest of the upper gallery took up the chant; eventually a reluctant Harlem appeared on stage to acknowledge the applause. In stark black, as usual, he appeared almost white-faced under the glare of the lights, the hollows under his cheekbones deeply shadowed as if the strain of the last few days had brought him close to exhaustion, and Tiffany tried not to stare at him too hard, though she knew he wouldn't be able to see her beyond the footlights.

He presented an elegant bunch of red roses, with the longest stems she had ever seen, to Lana as principal female dancer, and a whimsical bunch of violets to Maurice as the leading male. Then someone from the audience scrambled on to the stage and presented Harlem himself with one pure white chrysanthemum. The audience went wild, and, when they finally allowed the company to depart, the stage was littered with tokens of appreciation.

'Crazy!' exclaimed Ginny. 'Is it always like this?'

'Not in rehearsal, no.' Tiffany brought a smile to her face, veiling how her mind flitted back to that very different mood at yesterday's rehearsal when she and Harlem had faced each other out.

'My sculpture studio's going to seem very tame after this,' chattered Ginny as they went backstage. 'And I'd no idea Harlem was so raunchy. He's a living doll!'

'Join the fan club,' exclaimed a girl from the line, as she bumped into them outside her dressing-room and overheard Ginny's remarks. Ginny fell on her like a soul-sister. 'What it must be like to work with him!' she exclaimed. 'I'd give my right arm!'

The girl, Chrissy, shot a look at Tiffany. 'We survive, don't we?' Then she walked along with them. 'He treats us all with a sort of courteous disdain outside rehearsals, making sure we can pay our rent, get three square meals a day and have plenty of early nights. He listens patiently to our emotional problems and doles out useful advice if asked. None of us get near him; it's most frustrating. He's like nothing so much as a distant father figure! Isn't that so, Tiffany?'

Tiffany blushed, remembering the anything but fatherly way he had taken her lips that day on the roof. She nodded non-committally, and changed the subject, asking, 'I hope the set's not going to get knocked about if everybody's partying all over it.'

'They've decided to go on the terrace instead,' Chrissy told them. 'Come on!'

The sultry weather had held, and as they surged through Harlem's apartment on to the roof terrace beneath its canopy of stars there were murmurs of appreciation at the romantic scene that met them. The backstage staff had gone to town, rigging up coloured awnings at intervals between the skylights and filling them with braided cushions to create a setting of Arabian Nights' enchantment. A buffet feast was spread in gaudy array under ropes of lanterns at one end, and a space was set aside for the inevitable dancing later on. Playing their part to the hilt, the tech. men had donned Turkish djellabahs, and they swept down with trays of lethal-coloured cocktails as soon as the guests arrived.

'I shall overload with ecstasy when Harlem himself appears in the middle of all this,' whispered Ginny, pinching Tiffany's arm. She gave her friend a careful look. Tiffany had briefly told her about Harlem's wish to remain uninvolved and their argument the day before. 'Don't worry, pet, we'll all protect you from the big bad wolf.'

'Unfortunately that's not the kind of protection I need.' Tiffany's smile concealed her heartbreak. Just being here again told her there was only one way out. The conviction had started from anger, but it had been growing since yesterday and now she decided she would speak to Harlem alone if she got the chance and tell him what was on her mind.

When he eventually made his appearance it was as obvious as if heralded by drums and trumpets. A *frisson* of excitement seemed to ripple over the crowd and heads turned towards its source as Harlem picked his way on to the roof. Even though he worked alongside most of these people every day it was obvious to everyone that there was something different about him now, setting him further apart. It vibrated with a tangible force like a kind of sexual hunger only just reined in. All the tension of putting the show together had been released, and he strolled across his domain with his entourage of beautiful girls like a sultan visiting his harem after a long abstinence.

Tiffany shivered and tried to draw back into the purple shadows beneath the awning, but his restless eyes sought her out at once.

'No roses for Miss Mulgrove?' he asked ironically. Turning, he plucked a single stem from the bouquet Lana carried and, with an elegant gesture, tossed it on to her lap. Then, deliberately—she could see the glint of challenge in his eyes—he raised the glass of clear liquid he held and drained it. She turned away, but he hadn't finished with her yet.

Proceeding beneath the awning with his followers, he lowered himself on to a stage throne which the props men had brought up, and Tiffany found herself forced to look up at him from the cushions on which she reclined with her own small entourage. Then Harlem's eyes lazed over her face and began to slide in knowing provocation over the rest of her. She felt her insides quicken. As if he knew, he gave a smoky laugh, eyes never lifting from their slow journey.

As someone put another drink into his hand he said, 'Thank God no two bodies are the same! Think of the boredom!' When everyone stopped to listen he went on, 'Take Miss Mulgrove, for example.' Tiffany felt all eyes turn. 'To some she might appear to be a little overweight——' Lana tittered, but he went on without lifting his glance. 'While to others she might embody the ideal of fair womanhood, the perfect female form, with ravishing breasts, wide hips, and a handspan waist; an odalisque built for sensual dalliance, the voluptuous ideal of artists throughout the ages . . .' He paused. 'Isn't that so, Miss Mulgrove?'

Tiffany wished the floor would swallow her up. The very roots of her hair tingled with the old antagonism. But her throat closed and she could think of no reply to match the insulting lightness of his assessment. 'Heavens,' whispered Ginny in her ear, 'he says things out loud the boys in college couldn't even dream in private! I thought you said he didn't want to be involved?'

'He's trying to make me look a fool in front of everyone,' replied Tiffany in a tight voice. She scrambled to her feet but had to pass by Harlem's throne to get away, and as she did so he reached out and in a voice only she could hear asked, 'Where are you going?'

'What the hell's it got to do with you?' She tried to snatch her hand away from where he had clamped it beneath his own, but he only gripped it more fiercely and said, 'How did it look out front tonight?'

'Fantastic. You know it did.'

His lips relaxed a fraction. 'Thank you.'

Their eyes locked and for a moment out of time Tiffany felt the world revolve around that pinbright spot where they met before she wrestled her arm free.

'Wait—I'm coming with you!' He reached for his stick, but she twisted through the crowd, slipping hastily out of sight before he could stop her, praying he would be unable to follow.

She reached the cool green passage leading to the kitchen before she heard him call her name.

'It's no good, Harlem.' She turned, flattening herself against the wall as he tapped with his stick along the passage towards her. In the distance there was the sound of music and laughter, a conga line starting to weave across the roof.

'What do you mean, it's no good?' He was level with her now, his dark eyes raking her face, one hand coming out to pin her to the wall.

'I mean I have to hand in my notice—I'm asking to be released from my contract.'

'Impossible.'

'It's no good living like this. I guess I'm not hard-boiled enough to be able to work with you.' She took a gulping breath, already aware of how his presence was turning her limbs to water. 'You think people are clockwork. And it may work when it comes to running a dance company, but in any other world it's killing . . .'

His face was white, perspiration suddenly standing out on his forehead, and his eyes seemed to bore into her soul.

She put up a hand to try to move his fingers from her shoulder but his weight was against her and she let his hand lie there. 'It doesn't help to know you've had too much vodka,' she muttered, aware of the heavy intake and outflow of his breath as he drank her in.

'And by the time this night's over I may have yet more.' He gave a harsh laugh. 'What an unimaginative little puritan you are, Miss

Mulgrove, underneath your superficial creative self! And now I find you're walking out as soon as you hit a winning streak. How like a woman! You've no edge, baby. Don't you see? We're a winning team. And you're going to spoil it on a whim.'

'I've nothing else to say to you, Harlem.' She closed her eyes, only wanting to shut him out till the pain subsided, but she felt his fingers grip her chin and raise her face to his.

'Tiffany, listen to me.' His voice had thickened, forcing her to open her eyes. 'Understand this,' he breathed. 'To me you are light and life and vitality. Your youth is very precious. Don't squander it, do you hear me?' In a voice like torn silk he asked, 'Do you imagine I want to drag you down into the darkness with me?'

Slowly her eyes focused on his. There was no pretence in them; his soul was stripped bare. She could read only the anguish there, not the reason for it.

'Why do you say that, Harlem? What darkness? Why can't you see the wonderful thing you've created here? Why isn't it enough? It would be enough for me!'

He let his hand drop. His own eyelids closed for a fraction and his lips tightened in a cruel line. His voice was hoarse as he said, 'You'll never know what black monsters dwell within my mind, my dear one.' He lifted his head, and there was such a spasm of agony on his face Tiffany felt her heart lurch with pity.

'What is it, Harlem? What can ever be so bad? Isn't it time to forget the past now?'

As if coming to a sudden decision he gripped her by the wrist and, as the conga line came laughing and swaying down the corridor towards them, he dragged her along into the relative peace of the main room. Without saying anything he swung across to the other side and snatched up one of the photographs from the table, thrusting it into her hands with a look of black rage. It was the picture of the boy-child with the garland of roses she had seen before. 'See that? Does it look like the face of a murderer?' he ground out. 'Because it is!'

He snatched up another one. 'And this? See her? That dazzling innocence, that beauty— all gone! Finished!'

In a daze Tiffany stared at the photograph she had already seen, of the teenage boy and the ethereal girl in white tulle.

'I don't understand——' She held the photographs to her breasts, staring at Harlem in confusion.

He snatched the photographs and smashed them down on the table with such force the glass cracked. 'I killed her!' he rasped. 'That beautiful girl—together with her two companions.' His eyes held a wild black look as he went on. 'I was the driver of the car they

were travelling in. I killed them all—
Minoushka, her fiancé and another young
dancer from the same company. They were
all three people of rare talent. At the peak of
their careers. I killed them, Tiffany.' His voice
thickened and he said quickly. 'I shall never
learn to live with it, so don't tell me I'll get
over it. What happened to me myself is
nothing. I'm alive!' He thumped his chest in
despair. 'But I can tell you that as I lay in
that hospital bed I wished I could die. I
prayed for it. It seemed the only just thing.
And when I discovered I was going to survive
despite my prayers, I made up my mind to
dedicate the rest of my life to making
amends.' He laughed harshly. 'As if it would
ever be possible to balance out in good works
what I had so carelessly destroyed!'

Before she could say anything he gave her
one hard look, then turned and began to limp
across the room towards the roof terrace.

'Harlem!' Suddenly coming to life, she tore
after him, reaching him as he started up the
steps. 'Please, Harlem!' She gripped his arm.
'Don't shut me out, please. I——' With a
desperate cry she lifted her arms, feeling him
move towards her as her own body found his.
'Darling, please——' There were tears in her
eyes. 'Don't punish yourself like this. You
deserve love, too . . .'

She felt him hold her, holding her off, and
she moved more possessively against him,

cradling his dark head, pressing herself in desperation against him. He tightened his grip around her waist, squeezing hard, still managing to hold her back so that their bodies skimmed, scarcely touching. His eyes were unfathomable, but his voice was edged with self-mockery when he said, 'I guess I'm still adept at reducing an audience to tears. You should have seen me in *Petrushka*.'

She thought he was going to turn her away, but with a muffled groan the mockery left his face and he crushed her in his arms, fire bursting between them as contact was made at last. She felt his hands slide along the warm flesh below the waistband of her harem pants and splay the wide hips he had commented on before.

'I can't cope with two public performances in one night,' he muttered hoarsely after a moment, as their kisses became more fevered. 'Tiffany, my beauty, come . . . will you come to me? I need you so much. I can't fight forever.'

Without waiting for a reply, he reached for his stick, clamped her in his bulging arms and used her automatic support across the room into the corridor. The conga line was already on its way back and passed them in a blur of laughing faces. Tiffany felt she was in a dream. Only Harlem's touch whirling her into the stratosphere was real.

She heard a door open, felt the uncertainty of a darkened room beyond, and sank trustingly down within his arms, lying back where he tenderly guided her, discovering with a little moan of surrender a bed, pillows, silk, and the pulsing body of the man she loved coming urgently down over her own.

Their struggles matched in intensity as the restraints of belts and buttons and hampering garments were put aside, then with no other prelude he bent to cup her breasts, tasting the honeyed flesh with a savage hunger that brought an answering cry from deep within her. She arched as his mouth branded her with the marks of possession, twining her limbs around his own as he sank at once within her liquid heat, driving her with each thrust into a wordless zone of paradise, until in a moment the universe exploded in a consummation that was a pure dance of love. She cried his name over and over, again and again.

'I love you,' she said. 'I love you, Harlem. Love me. Love me forever . . .' Her murmured cries faded in a haze of pleasure as her body was teased again by the magic of new sensations bringing her to life. She moaned with renewed pleasure as he took her boneless limbs under his masterly control, playing an expert symphony of unimaginable delight that brought her breathlessly to a zenith of expectation again. Then, holding her at a point beyond any pleasure she had ever dreamed of, he began

to teach her the rhythms of a *pas de deux* that
tore her body into a thousand splinters of joy.

'Tiffany,' he muttered, 'no other woman
has ever got through to me as you have. Help
me. I can't live with it. I have to set you free.
Understand me, my dear, heavenly love . . .
it's tearing at my soul. There's no way out.'

'Harlem, do whatever you want with me. I
belong to you. But, as long as you'll live,
you'll never set me free.' She ran her fingers
tenderly over the bulging muscles of his back,
taking possession of them with every sortie
like an explorer in a new land. 'I love you,'
she confessed. 'I surrender to you. I'm your
willing prisoner, yours forever.' She reached
up in the darkness to touch the blur of the
face that hovered over hers, feeling with joy
the fullness of the lips she had longed to own.
'I've dreamed of your mouth so often,
Harlem. Your beautiful mouth.' Her fingers
feathered over it, 'Touch me, love. Love me,
love me, Harlem . . .'

And he began to place his mouth, the
mouth she had yearned so long for, all over
her heated body in places she had never
suspected it could go . . .

'Tell me the darkness is over,' she whispered
incautiously, as she raked his back with her
fingers. 'Please, my love, tell me it's all over . . .'

His self-control cracked under her touch,
and again he thrust into her, matching her
cries with his own as his will gave way and

the world exploded around them once more.

Harlem touched her after that in ways she had never imagined, and she became his willing slave, an odalisque in the private harem of one to whom pleasure was the rule. All the night long he taught her how to touch a man to make him cry out in surrender, and in return he transported her to the peaks of a sublime consummation.

After this night of nights, she thought, as, hours later, dawn stole through the uncurtained windows, life can never be the same. She felt she had touched the core of living as she lifted her head and let her hungry eyes travel over the sleeping form of the man lying beside her.

'Harlem,' she whispered, showering his sleeping face with kisses, joying in the touch of her lips against the delicious warmth of his skin, and melting again as she felt the magic quicken between them. 'Harlem, my love . . .'

He stirred in sleep. She felt his lashes brush her cheek as his eyes opened. 'Darling Tiffany.' He pulled her face against his, rippling the long hair through his fingers. 'Don't love me too much. Please, angel. Not too much.'

'Harlem, what can ever be too much?' She raised her head, squirming to look up into his face. 'Harlem?' Her tone changed, something deep in his eyes making her shudder. 'I can't help myself,' she told him.

'No!' His voice broke. 'Don't, please, Tiffany . . . Oh, hell, I lost control last night. After fighting to keep you at arm's length for so long! No other woman has ever got through in quite this way before . . .!' He pushed her aside and swung his legs over the edge of the bed, looking back at her with a glance that at once made her sit upright. He dashed away the hand she put out.

'Tiffany, what the hell came over me? Listen, you're sweet and lovely and adorable. But you mustn't even *think* of me. I'm not the one for you. You deserve so much more. I'm a mess, believe me!'

'No, Harlem! You're all I could ever want!'

He seemed to summon up a cold strength, drawing it inwards, his face draining of life with the effort, and in a flush of dismay she saw him rise to his feet and drag on a pair of jeans and a shirt without a glance at her. Galvanised by his apparent indifference, she sprang out of bed and flew to his side. 'What are you doing?' she gasped. 'Are you leaving me?'

'Tiffany, please! Let me be!' He shook her hand off and reached for his stick.

'Harlem!' she shrieked as he started for the door.

'Get away, Tiffany. What more do you want? Haven't you had enough?' His black eyes swept her with a look that made her tremble. 'I can't give you anything else! There's nothing left! You were right when you said I was a zero inside! I lost control, that's all! Now forget it!'

With a muffled curse he turned for the door.

In a fever of despair she saw him drag it open. From the terrace came the distant sounds of last night's music, the clink of glasses and subdued laughter telling her the party was still going on.

'Where are you going?' she screamed. 'Don't leave me now!' In a fever she ran towards him. 'Who are you going to?' she cried, desperation making her fingers claw at his arm.

He gave her one slow, sorrowing look. 'Never that, Tiffany. If I went to any woman it would always be to you.' He held her arm so tightly she flinched, but refused to withdraw. Then with a final, deliberate, raking glance, he turned her face up to his, eyes probing every tell-tale sign of love in it. 'What have I done?' he groaned. 'Forgive me ... and forget me!'

Before she could hold him back he swung away, feeling his way along the corridor, and only the sound of the outer door banging behind him told her he was going beyond her reach.

Snatching up a robe from a chair, she flew after him, her bare feet pattering on the cold tiles of the corridor, her breath coming in short snatches as she threw herself down the stairs.

He was already in the foyer when she finally caught up with him but, with only a rough command to stay where she was, he went out of the stage door and down the steps into the street while she stood shivering in the cold air with the thin robe still clutched around her nakedness.

She dashed a hand through tangled hair. 'Harlem!' she called again from the top of the steps. 'Wait!'

'Get back! There's no other way!'

She saw him limp across the pavement to where Frank's silver Jaguar was perched by the kerb, and he turned to look back when he reached it, a grimace tracing over his face as he thrust a hand into his pocket and held up a bunch of keys. 'Tell him, will you? He's been trying to persuade me to do it for long enough.'

Before she could take in what he was saying, he was sliding into the driver's seat and switching on the ignition, and then she gave a cry of fear when she saw the expression on his face. She stumbled down the steps, oblivious to the fact that she was in bare feet and dressed only in a thin robe, but even as she ran across the pavement the engine snarled into life, and the car began to slide away from the kerb, gathering speed like a silver bullet as it tore down the street, and she had to stand helplessly as he drove off into the pearly dawn.

Her emotions were in turmoil as she ran back up the stairs to the penthouse and dragged on a few clothes. After all that he had told her through the night she knew this was no ordinary drive. Her nerves were stretched like overwound bowstrings as she went in search of Frank. He was sitting alone by the parapet, watching the sun come up.

'Frank!' She needed only to say his name before he opened his arms to her.

Sliding out of his brief embrace, she crouched on one of the Turkish cushions at his feet. 'It's Harlem,' she began brokenly, rocking back and forth. 'He's taken your car. Oh, my God, what can we do!' Suddenly all the tension inside dissolved in a spout of tears and she felt Frank's arms come round her again, forcing her to look at him.

'What did he tell you?' he demanded hoarsely.

'He didn't make sense. He's driven off in your car, Frank. What does it mean?'

'Damn my car. I don't care about that. I care about him. What did he say?'

'He said a lot of things. He blames himself for everything. He said you'd been trying to persuade him long enough—to drive?' she asked, looking up. Frank nodded, and she went on 'What does it mean, Frank? What have I done?'

'Don't blame yourself,' he told her tersely, rocking her back and forth in his arms. 'It had to happen, sooner or later ... Did he say where he was going?'

She shook her head.

'Don't blame yourself,' he said again. 'He'll be all right. The car's an automatic, so his leg's no problem. It's something he had to face.' He stroked the tousled hair and gazed into her violet eyes with great compassion. 'He still can't forgive himself for what happened,' he told her. 'He can't accept that it wasn't his fault.'

'What did happen, Frank?' she asked. 'He said he killed them ...'

'No, it was a design fault in the car he happened to be driving. But he won't listen to reason. He seems to think he should be able to control everything. He won't accept that sometimes even he can lose control through no fault of his own.'

Tiffany felt a shock wave go through her. 'Is that what he's fighting against?' she asked. 'Losing control?' Her mind went back to the desire that had swept aside all rational restraint that night. She blushed, then realising that Frank was wiser than she knew, muttered, 'He can't accept what happened last night ...' Her eyes were stricken when she raised them to his. 'What if he ...? What if ...?' The words were too ghastly to frame.

Frank took charge. 'He'll be back. I told

you, it's something he had to do sooner or later. He's refused to drive since the smash. But it's a challenge he has to face. He's got to learn that he can control most situations—but not all. No human being has ultimate control. That's something we all have to live with. He's got to learn how.'

They sat together for an hour as the sun came up on another hot day. Tiffany scarcely saw the glorious pinks and blues and amethysts as the sun's rays touched the city peaks to life. The roofs of London shone like silver discs in the pure light as the streets still slept before the roar of London's morning rush-hour shattered the calm.

When by eight o'clock the last of the revellers had departed she rose stiffly to her feet. 'I want to ring the hospitals,' she muttered. 'I can't bear to sit here doing nothing, uselessly waiting, just waiting . . .'

'No.' Frank detained her with a gentle hand. 'I know Harlem, my love. He's not the type to walk out on us.'

She knew he was right, but thanked him in the silence of her heart for the tactful way he phrased it. Walk out . . . she supposed making a final reckoning with life could be described that way.

Not a breath of air stirred the now sad awnings from the night before. The oppressive weather needed a storm to cleanse the air, but there was no hint of rain. Frank made coffee in the kitchen and brought it out on to the roof. Finally they went back indoors, sitting by unspoken agreement near the black telephone. The distant sounds of daytime London began to float up from the streets.

Frank was pale-faced now. 'He's seen me through thick and thin,' he told her. 'He's one of the very best. You won't know about the scholarship fund he set up as soon as he started to hit the big time?' She shook her head. 'That's not all. He supports a village in India. He finances three schools in various parts of the world, and he's planning a new school of dance here in the East End like the one he founded in the Bronx.'

'I'd no idea he did any of this,' she told him.

'He likes to keep it quiet. That's his way.'

He got up restlessly and went out on to the roof. When he returned his face was grey. 'The trouble is he can't accept the shadow side,' he told her. 'He wants to feel he has the power of life over death. He won't accept the finality of it. He believes art transcends it and so can he. If he would only accept that he's human like the rest of us . . .'

'If only he could accept that—he'd be able to accept my love as a sort of redemption, wouldn't he?' she said in a rush of understanding.

CHAPTER NINE

LOOKING back on that morning and the hours that stretched like a long agony until Harlem's call came, Tiffany wondered how she had managed to summon the strength to keep going. Only the days that followed subjected her to a more harrowing test, when Harlem's continued absence seemed to tear her flesh with a physical torment. He didn't come back, but at least they knew he was safe.

His first call had come later that morning, from Scotland. 'I've taken your advice, Frank, and given your car a really good outing. Now the show's safely on the road,' went on the metallic voice from all those miles away, 'they can get along without me.'

Frank lifted his head from the receiver. 'Tiffany's here, Shall I—?'

She heard the response, saw Frank's mouth tighten with embarrassment and turned away, not wanting to hear excuses. Afterwards Frank told her to take one day at a time. 'He's never given himself the opportunity to come to terms with what's happened. He's not himself. He'll be back when he's ready . . .'

A few days later, though, Harlem called Frank from New York. Some administrative problem at the school required his presence.

A week later it was India. A call to
Marguerite on finance. July came to a close,
still without word for Tiffany.

Frank encouraged her to assist him on
some designs for an experimental work by a
small opera company. 'It's right up your
street,' he told her. 'I need somebody under
twenty-five with a fresh eye.'

'You're very sweet, Frank.' She did her best,
going into the studio every day as if everything
were all right, working at her workbench, going
home at night, acting out the motions of
someone in control. But in reality she was like
one of the walking wounded.

At the beginning of August she took two
weeks' holiday on Ibiza with Ginny and a
few others, and what she had begun to
suspect was confirmed when she returned to
London and booked an appointment at an
anonymous clinic off Oxford Street. She
submitted to counselling both for and against
giving life to Harlem's child. In her mind she
knew there was no doubt what she would do.
Her career might be on the line, but the
thought of the life inside her, flesh of his
flesh, swept aside any doubts she had. In the
circumstances there was no real choice at all.

She made a visit to Fareham, and told her
parents as calmly as she could what had
happened and what she intended to do. They
didn't try to persuade her one way or the other,

trusting her judgement, and shortly afterwards she received an encouraging letter from Fay in Manchester. Ginny and Pat were still on holiday, and she was relieved she had no more explaining to do just yet and had the house to herself. Each evening she spent endless hours sitting by the window, staring out at the sunlit streets, wondering what he was doing, where he was, who he was with—and if that dark pain had finally receded.

The morning sickness started early, and she found it more and more difficult to drag herself into the studio on time. Only by throwing herself into her work when she was there could she manage to keep going. Frank, too sensitive to let much get past, commented on her pallor.

'You overdoing it, sweetheart?' he asked casually one lunchtime, as they sat in the pub round the corner from the studio. For once Jason and Gavin were absent on some mission elsewhere.

'I'm fine,' she lied, but she could tell from the brief flare of colour and the sheepish look she had been unable to control that Frank was unconvinced.

'He's coming back in a few days,' he told her towards the end of that week. 'Has he been in touch?'

She shook her head.

Frank's expression hardened. 'OK . . . Do you want me to tell him anything?'

She shook her head again. 'It's up to him now, isn't it?'

'You'll have to see him some time,' he admonished gently. 'You can't play hide and seek with each other forever.'

Tiffany bowed her head. She knew Frank was right. 'It's up to him,' she repeated stubbornly. 'It's fate.' She tried to smile.

She could tell as soon as she walked into the studio a few days later that Harlem was back. The atmosphere had changed. Jason and Gavin, guessing something had happened between him and Tiffany, echoed Frank's manner of walking on eggshells.

Tiffany didn't expect to see him so soon. It was a shock therefore when, as she slipped out to the shops mid-morning to buy some of the mint humbugs she had developed a craving for, she saw him as he was just coming down the steps of the theatre. Their glances alighted on each other at the same moment and their steps simultaneously jerked to a stop. Harlem was the first to recover. He strolled slowly across the pavement towards her.

'Hi! Fancy meeting you.'

She had imagined this moment so many times, and now she could only stare dumbly into his eyes for a sign of a wild spasm of joy like that which leaped within her at the sight of him now. It was so violent she wondered if it showed on her face as the tongue of flame it felt like within. Apparently not, she thought, as Harlem gave a shrug and looked as if he was about to continue down the street.

'You've been away a long time,' blurted out Tiffany, saying anything to detain him.

'I needed a rest,' he told her abruptly. 'I'd got to breaking point without realising it. Those damned medics were probably right about taking time off. Still, better late than never.' He still had the stick, and now he poked about between the paving stones with it. 'How are you?' He looked up. 'Getting on well with Frank?'

She nodded. 'He's asked me to work on some new opera designs. It's fun,' she added, wondering if the inexorable passage of the last few weeks could rightly be described that way.

'Good. I thought he'd snap you up, given the chance.' His dark eyes raked her face. 'I take it your resignation was definite, then?'

Her eyes opened wide. 'No, I haven't been thinking of it like that——'

'It's all right,' he interrupted. 'I don't mind releasing you. It's obviously for the best. Frank rated you highly from the start.'

'He won't mind if I work on your new autumn show,' she said hastily.

'I wouldn't dream of poaching you back into the fold.' He had a tan now from all his travelling, but his face was greyish and Tiffany wanted to reach up to him, take him in her arms and talk to him, and listen to him telling her things the way she knew lovers should. But he bulked so large, with such an air of dark rage about him, that her courage failed and she didn't know how to begin to let him know all that was in her heart. And in the brief pause when she could have made a move she hesitated just a fraction too long and the moment was gone.

'I'll be getting along then.' He swivelled abruptly, and she watched him swing off rapidly down the street to the corner. When he was out of sight she gazed dumbly at the space on the pavement where he had stood.

After that brief meeting she saw no more of Harlem for the rest of the week, and just before leaving on Friday afternoon she broached the question of her contract with Frank.

'I'm not sure what I'm supposed to do,' she said, trying to keep her lips from trembling. 'I thought I had a contract with Harlem, but he says he'll be willing to release me if you— if you . . .'

'All right,' Frank squeezed her shoulder. 'It's time somebody had a word with the great Barensky.'

'Frank, please don't——' She swallowed. 'Please don't say anything—about anything not to do with work, I mean . . .' She blinked and turned away. 'I don't want any favours.'

'Favours?' Frank looked as if he was about to explode, but when Tiffany swung back and clutched his arm, pleading, he shook his head wonderingly. 'Just what's with you two?' he asked. But he didn't press it. And when she made him promise he gave a shrug of resignation.

The first time she knew that Frank had got round to saying anything at all was on Monday morning when, deeply engrossed in the construction of a tiny model of the opera house stage, she heard the outer door of the studio bang inwards. Frank was out, and until the studio door itself was flung open she assumed the noise was him on his way back in. Continuing without looking up, she was startled when a long buff envelope landed with a thud on the table in front of her.

'That what you want?' grated a voice in her ear. 'You might have had the courtesy to come and ask me for it yourself!'

She raised her head to find Harlem's dark eyes confronting her. Satisfied that he had said all he wanted, he turned as if to go.

'Harlem!' She rose to her feet, grappling on the table for the envelope and slitting it open with shaking fingers as she ran after him to the door. A glance at the typewritten pages told her all she needed to know. 'Wait, you've got to hear me,' she whispered, conscious of interested glances from across the studio.

'I've heard all I want to hear.' His eyes swept her face and then, perhaps because he saw something there he hadn't expected, his manner softened. He halted with his hand on the door, adding, 'It's just that I thought you were in two minds about leaving me. Then this.' He gestured towards the contract. 'I guess your reticence was just your natural English good manners.'

'I've never been in two minds about leaving you, Harlem. Either I've wanted to leave you—desperately. Or I've wanted to stay.'

'Desperately?' A corner of his mouth lifted a fraction.

For a moment her glance held his. Then she gave a slight nod.

'And what mood is it today, I wonder?' He lifted his dark head, gazing full into her face before turning with an irritable shake. He looked out through the half-open door, and Tiffany saw the struggle he was having with some inner force.

'Did Frank tell you I wanted to leave my job with you?' she asked, choosing her words carefully.

'Not exactly. I put two and two together.' He swung back. 'The fact that you haven't been over to see what's on the stocks seemed to make plain enough what you were trying to tell me.'

She felt her heart begin to move with something like the fluttering of reawakened hope. 'I didn't know I was supposed to come over—that I'd be welcome,' she faltered.

He sighed. 'I seem to remember this happening once before. It's obviously your habit to play hard to get——'

'Hardly.' She smiled faintly. His eyes narrowed as he saw what was in her mind. Just standing next to him was doing strange things to her and she couldn't help noticing that the anger that had suffused his face when he first made his entrance had given way to another, gentler mood.

As if to confirm it he reached out, picked the contract from her hands and, holding it between two fingers, raised his eyebrows. 'No?'

'No.' She shook her head.

Resting his stick against the door, he tore the foolscap pages into shreds and handed them back to her. 'You'd better report for duty as soon as possible, Miss Mulgrove. There's a new show to design.' He gave a mocking glance at the baggy T-shirt she had on. 'You still believe in making the imagination do overtime, I see,' he commented, and before he left he added, 'I'm willing to share you with Frank until you've finished his opera for him, but after that . . . you have to be all mine.'

As the door clicked shut Tiffany felt a stab in her womb, his words echoing and re-echoing, hinting at more than he explicitly uttered, but she controlled her hurtling desires with an effort. A day at a time, she told herself. We're talking now without flying at each other's throats. In a little while we'll talk as lovers should.

* * *

Bearing in mind Harlem's comment about her baggy T-shirt, she reported for work two days later in a wide floral skirt and white blouse, cinched together with a broad blue leather belt, and, always aware of how he seemed to dwarf her, she slipped on a pair of high-heeled leather sandals in a matching shade of blue. The summer sun had turned her legs to a golden sheen, and as she stood in front of the mirror before setting out she noticed that the pallor of a few weeks ago was beginning to give way to a subtle bloom that added a lustre to her skin, setting off her startling violet eyes which these days held an added depth of womanhood. Even her hair seemed to have improved, she registered, its usual gleaming silk even more lustrous. With it swirling in a dark mist over her shoulders she felt prepared for the sort of glance Harlem would subject her to when they came face to face at last.

'All right, Mr Barensky,' she said to herself as she stood outside the door to his penthouse. 'Here I come.'

Anya let her in, gesturing to the far room and patting Tiffany's arm as she pushed her towards it with a stream of friendly Russian. Then she disappeared into the kitchen, and Tiffany made her way as calmly as she could over the cool green tiles to the door at the end of the corridor.

Harlem was bending over a collection of

tapes when she opened the door. He glanced over his shoulder, saying, when he saw who it was, 'Listen to this. Dance number one. Untitled,' and then he swung round as the first notes of a bitter-sweet melody flooded the room. He opened his mouth to speak, then closed it again.

Tiffany for her part stood in the doorway, suddenly shocked into the knowledge that he still desired her, her own wild yearnings swooping to meet his and heightened by the liquid melody as the music grew in volume, as if to carry them both beyond the moment into some other realm.

Harlem himself broke the spell. Turning with a sudden shake of his head, he snapped off the power control. 'Damn it, let's——' He turned back to her, his glance avoiding hers, shouting suddenly, 'Anya? Let's have some coffee in here!' He limped rapidly over to the door, and Tiffany moved out of the way as he called into the corridor in a flood of unintelligible Russian.

'Sit down,' he said tersely when he turned back. 'Maybe it'll be best if I give you the notes first, then you can borrow the tapes and listen to them at home. I'—he glanced around as if looking for something then flicked a look at his watch—'I have to go out in about half an hour. But we can talk through the notes briefly over coffee. You have a decent cassette player at home, I suppose?'

She nodded, confused by the sudden chill in his manner.

He thrust a folder into her hand. 'Scan that. I'll see how Anya's getting on.' Before she could say anything he had left the room. He didn't return for quarter of an hour, by which time Tiffany had managed to pull herself together, riffle through the notes and arrange her expression to a cool shell as he came back in.

He placed the tray on a low table between them and took his place on the brocade and gilt chair.

'Does it interest you?' he asked, not looking at her but pouring out two cups of thick black coffee with careful concentration.

'That's a silly question.' From what she had read it was a wildly tragic piece, only lightened by a manic sequence of ribald humour two-thirds of the way through. But despite its intended fevour it was sure box-office. The music, she noticed from the notes, was modern, blues, jazz, reggae, salsa, with a sequence of blatantly experimental stuff by a young American composer thrown in for good measure.

'Dante's *Inferno*,' he informed her, looking everywhere but in her face. 'Transported into the twentieth century. I thought it might be an amusing transposition.'

'Amusing?'

He got up and moved awkwardly to the

window, and she thought he was going to go out on to the terrace but he stopped there in the doorway, his back towards her. 'I'm glad you can be mature about this—working together, I mean. We're a good team and it would be a shame to throw that away just because we happened to lose control one night.' He turned back and his face was in shadow against the lighter colour of the London sky. 'I don't want to go over the edge with you again—I can't risk losing myself in you. I know you understand how important that is to me.'

Tiffany felt her fingers close over the sheaf of notes, and with an effort she forced herself to relax them. 'If you give me the tapes I'll go back now and listen to them,' she told him without a waver in her voice. 'Can you give me a day or two to come up with something? Or do you expect instant results?' Is this me? she thought, as she heard herself give a light laugh.

'Good girl.' He seemed to relinquish a large boulder of tension from his shoulders. 'The day after tomorrow?'

She nodded.

'And, Tiffany, do turn up. I seem to spend my life wondering where you are.'

If only you did, she thought as she finished her coffee, then maybe it would mean you felt the same way about me as I do about you. That flare of desire in his eyes when she came in must have been just that—the sexual desire of an easily aroused male for an attractive woman. She could have been anybody. His deliberate distancing told her as plainly as words that he felt nothing more.

After an agonising day and night sitting glued to the cassette player while the others were out Tiffany felt she had been on an excursion to hell and back. Reading his notes and listening again and again to the music to get the mood of his *Inferno* piece just right, she realised that it sprang from that black stratum of pain deep inside him that had sent him driving off into the dawn those weeks ago. Now she saw with blinding clarity that it had been grief, not bitterness, that had infused his mind. And it was equally obvious he had somehow risen about the pain, moulding it into a work of art that would move audiences even if they could not share directly in its source. She switched off the recording for the ninth time, and lay back with closed eyes. This was the next best thing to being with him, she supposed, sharing in the patterns of his mind.

It was ten o'clock when she arrived at the theatre and made her way up to his apartment with a folder bulging with notes.

'Hi!' Harlem was standing at the top of the stairs looking down, and called to her as she began the ascent.

She looked up and then away, shakily conscious that his eyes never left her as she went up. When she reached the top he was draped across the door, one arm resting on the frame. She felt he had been waiting there for the sound of the door for some time.

'I hope I'm not late,' she greeted. The sickness seemed to be receding, but this morning had been one of those off-days and she had taken longer than expected to get herself together. She wore a white dress, one of her old ones, and the blue leather belt. It had had to be let out a notch, but apart from that she felt unchanged. It was almost as if nothing was happening.

He gave her that old smile, all brilliance and mockery. 'You're blooming this morning, Miss Mulgrove. September suits you.' Turning, he walked unevenly back into the sitting-room. 'So what have you got for me?'

'You're a real slave-driver,' she said to his back, wanting to savour his presence before the considerations of work pushed everything else to one side.

'Ivan the Terrible? Isn't that what they call me behind my back?'

'Among other things,' she teased, her glance fastening on the wide mouth as he turned. She felt something sweep through her like a flood of molten honey, and to hide what her eyes must reveal she went over to the table and threw down her files. 'There you are.'

He came up behind her. 'Where are the tapes?'

'In my bag.' She reached for them, and then shuddered as his fingers grazed hers as she handed them over.

He turned, as if intending to feed them into the machine, but she stepped forward. 'Don't do that—we both know them backwards by now.' The thought of having to listen to them all over again, conscious of what had been going through her mind during the last two days, was more than she could bear. He gave her a puzzled glance but switched the machine off.

'Where's Anya today?' she asked as he moved back to the table and flipped open the top file.

'Day off,' he told her, not looking up.

Tiffany went over to the french doors and gazed out over the roof terrace as he went through her notes. Dried leaves had somehow managed to get themselves carried up here from the trees in the square below. Summer was really over now.

When she turned back he was sprawled over the chesterfield, papers spread around him, a pencil stuffed behind one ear, an expression of marked concentration on his face, but as she came near he looked up. There was a smile on his face. 'You are clever. I do love you.' And, before she could process the phrase he had just used, he went on without a pause. 'If you'd insisted on leaving the outfit I think I would probably have come around to pleading with you to stay.'

'For the good of—the good of the company, of course?' she managed to ask.

'Yes. The good of the company.' His voice deepened.

'Yes,' she said, turning, her eyes suddenly blinded by tears. 'I'd have liked to have seen that—you pleading!' She pretended to laugh.

'Tiffany?' When she turned back he was looking down at the neatly written pages; he tapped them with his forefinger without looking up, saying, 'Let's discuss this, shall we?'

She went to one of the high-backed chairs, dragging it across the floor, but when he saw what she was doing he said, 'You won't be able to see from there. Come and sit here.'

Her body quickened at the image of his body, taut with vitality, pressing accidentally against her own while he talked, unaware of what it was doing to her. By an effort of sheer will she managed to force herself to sit at the farthest edge from him, erect, crossing her ankles, forcing herself to endure such intimate agony in silence. He was already analysing her notes, offering suggestions, making sounds of approval as his eyes flew over the pages.

'I see you quarrel with my ideas for the close?' he said at last, looking up.

'It seemed so black,' she replied. 'I thought you might eventually revise it?'

'How?' he asked.

'Well, you let your hero stay in hell, but surely anyone, however guilty, can be redeemed by love?' Her eyes were a haze of violet as she dared to raise them.

He looked away. 'Do you think so? Do you really think so?' His voice seemed to come from far away.

'I know so. In reality life goes on. New life . . .' She hesitated. 'New life is born.'

He let the notes slide to the floor. 'I'll think about that.' She felt his hand reach out for her, dragging her across the space that still separated them. 'But now I want to think about you.'

'Don't, Harlem . . .'

'Your eyes. I never really forgot them,' he said huskily. 'Can't we be mature about this, Tiffany? I so want to love you, take you to my bed again, hold you, touch your breasts, kiss you——'

'In your bed? Love?'

'You know what I mean. Your body is a woman's body, ripe for love. Why deny it?'

'Love?' she repeated again.

'You know it can't be permanent between us. I daren't risk that. but I can be good to you for a while . . .'

She was about to pull away, aware that he couldn't know how his words seared her with the premonition of future absence, when she remembered how he had expected her to make the first move before. Knowing that the decision was in her own hands, she reached up, linking her hands behind his head. Her body pressed against his. It was better than nothing. She knew he wouldn't prevent her leaving whenever she wanted.

'Harlem,' she whispered. 'Let me make love to you.' Sooner than he could answer she began to unbutton the front of his shirt before she could lose her nerve, running her fingers quickly inside the opening to seek the warmth she so longed to feel. She noticed his eyes widen in surprise, then drop their defences. He gave a small groan of pleasure as her fingers teased inside his shirt and lying back with his eyes closed he began to surrender to her touch, guiding her hands to where they gave most pleasure, shifting slightly to make her task easier.

'Harlem,' she whispered, 'I think we should take our clothes right off. Are you sure no one can come in?'

'Door's on the latch,' he muttered. 'Just pull my shoes off for me . . .' He groaned as she slithered down the length of his outstretched body to reach them, and as she tugged them off he held her, one hand gripping her right hip, the other teasing under the hem of her dress till it found the moist centre of her desire.

'Your skin, Tiffany, it's like oiled silk, so

beautiful, so beautiful . . . you have never looked so beautiful, so rich, so ripe . . . so fertile . . . like a goddess . . .'

He tried to raise himself to bring his face against the light gold of her inner thighs, and she felt his fingers grapple with the buckle of her belt, releasing her from its constraints with a sigh of pleasure. then the garments of both of them rippled to the floor, and their limbs wrapped around each other as they themselves followed, sinking to the carpet.

His body, which she had learned by touch before, became a study in sight and taste. Her eyes followed the lines of his muscles, drinking in their shape, tracing with her lips the perfect line from shoulder to chest with a sort of rage of hunger as she felt him move against her. She murmured, 'You're so beautiful, Harlem. So big, so powerful . . . so utterly perfect.'

'Flawed, rather,' he answered, weaving his fingers through the dark streamers of her hair as it flowed over him, moving her lower.

She discovered the jagged scar that bisected his body from one side of his chest to his abdomen, kissing it along its fiery trail till it lost itself in the dark hairs below his navel.

Then his own lips began to draw a fevered response from her as she too yielded to the flame burning within him like a forest fire, his hands travelling over her silken limbs with all the urgency of need and drawing her beneath him as the tension mounted. His powerful body covered hers and began to drive her further and further towards a peak of rapture just beyond their reach. Gasping wildly against his chest, she was dragging him deeper towards her secret self, frantically drawing him over the edge with her, and then suddenly she was falling and they were toppling together through space, a cry of final surrender wrenched from his throat as they fell together, and the world burst into flames around them.

CHAPTER TEN

AS THE days of September mellowed in a
haze of harvest gold, work on the new
autumn show proceeded with all the speed
and manic concentration Tiffany had come
to expect from Harlem. His urgency was
contagious, and the company threw
themselves to the verge of exhaustion in a
desire to bring the show to perfection before
the general public could be allowed to see it.

By day Harlem was a tower of cool
strength, treating everyone with the same
impartial judgement, nursing and nurturing,
provoking and occasionally castigating the
members of his company, until their
performance was like a machine engineered
to perfection. Tiffany was only half aware of
the fever of rehearsal that was going on next
door, for, after she had completed her designs
for Harlem, Frank asked to borrow her again
and appeared determined to keep her hard
at work. She welcome the discipline with
relief, treating it as a means to a necessary
amnesia through the daylight hours, aware
that it was only at night that she became truly
alive.

For it was then that Harlem would turn to
her, fever in his eyes, a darkness in him that

was different from anything she had seen before. He made love to her like a man driven by some demon, drawing from her the sweetness stored only for him, surrendering himself to her in return with a desperation bordering on delirium. Their nights were incandescent, his touch making her shimmer with a love all the more strong for the secret harvest that was coming to season inside her. Knowing she could neither halt nor hasten it, she glowed with the knowledge of its slow fruition, returning only at dawn to her other, daytime self.

One day towards the end of the month, with the opening night less than twenty-four hours away, Harlem dragged her against him in the darkness backstage during a break in a rehearsal at which she was present for once. Against their unwritten code he slithered a fingertip inside the neck of her sweater, so that she could feel the fever vibrating through his fingertips as he traced the line of her collarbone.

'Did you adjust that ramp as I asked you to?' he demanded, making the alteration in her design a pretext for this sudden, secret exchange. And before she could answer his mouth swept down briefly over hers in a hard plundering of the sweetness reserved for the night hours.

'You know that's not what I really want to talk about,' he muttered hoarsely before she could reply, keeping his voice low as a burst of conversation penetrated the thin partition behind which they were standing. 'I can't go on like this, Tiffany, pretending by day, loving you only in secret at night. I'm like a man being torn in two. Move in with me for a week or so. Let me send a car round for your things tonight. Move in. Let's slake ourselves of this thirst once and for all.'

Tiffany put a hand to her mouth as if defending it against the further marauding of his lips, swaying with the fervour of his glance, a sudden wild, pulsing joy at the thought that she would be his both night and day leaping within her. But even as her heart drummed she knew it could never be. Before she had time to gather herself to tell him so, a voice called from the direction of the stage.

'Must go. I'll see you when we're through.' He planted another brief kiss on her forehead before she could reply. Then he was gone, banging on the stage with his stick— winding up the rest of his clockwork toys, she thought bitterly, as she glanced at the stage filling with dancers ready to leap to his command.

She made her way next door. Frank was painting a backdrop to some design with swift sure sweeps of his brush and didn't look up as she gathered her things together. 'You won't mind if I go off early, will you?' she called when her bench was clear.

He gave her a brief glance, attention still on his task. 'Fine, sweetheart. Going home to put your feet up?'

She nodded.

'See you in the morning then.'

Racked with guilt at her deception, she let herself out into the street, then took the long way home.

Ginny and Pat were going out to a meal and then on to a party that night, and when they were ready Ginny stood in the doorway of her bedroom and eyed Tiffany with concern. 'I feel as if I'm nagging to ask you this again, but I can easily stay with you if you'd rather,' she said. 'I don't mind about this party, honestly.'

'I'll be fine by myself, Ginny. I just feel like an early night. No need to spoil your fun.' By now they knew about the baby.

'It's him, isn't it? You still haven't told him, have you?'

'There's hardly any point. A permanent relationship is the last thing he wants. His idea of the future doesn't stretch further than his next opening night.' She bent to switch on the gas fire and shivered a little. 'If it's of any interest he asked me to move in with him "for a week or two", quote, unquote . . .'

'And?'

'That's why I came back early this afternoon. I just couldn't bear the thought of having to summon up the strength to fight him. I'm just too tired right now not to take the coward's way out.'

'You'll have to face him some time.'

'Not necessarily. His time's completely taken up with getting the show up. That gives me twenty-four hours' reprieve. By the end of which I shall be back home in Fareham. I've just rung my parents.' She lifted her head. 'You won't let him know where I've gone, will you?'

Ginny gave her a derisive look. 'I just hope you know what you're doing. He may not want to take no for an answer.'

'He'll have to, won't he? I couldn't bear to live with him under conditions like those. Knowing it was all just building up to the final goodbye.'

Ginny was reluctantly reassured by Tiffany's detached manner, and she and Pat left soon afterwards. It was still only about seven o'clock and Tiffany gathered a few things together to take home with her the next day, had a leisurely bath, and then really did decide to have an early night. She was just about to climb into bed when the phone rang. At once her nerves jangled in response, some sixth sense warning her it was Harlem. She went into the sitting-room and stood next to the phone, watching it fixedly as if the caller on the other end could hear her slightest movement, until the bell finally came to an abrupt stop.

Ten minutes later it rang again. And again fifteen minutes after that. She climbed out of bed then and buried the instrument under a mound of cushions, closing the adjoining door into the sitting-room to be on the safe side. Despite this she went to sleep almost as soon as her head hit the pillow.

It was a thunderous knocking on the street door that woke her next. Reaching out, she saw it was still only nine o'clock. Obviously everybody in the rest of the house was out, for no one answered the door, and Tiffany crouched under the bedclothes wondering if she dared creep over to the window and look out, just to make sure. She could hear a taxi's engine idling, and eventually she was relieved to hear it drive off down the road.

That should be that, she thought, mildly shocked at Harlem's persistence, and she let herself drift back into the pleasant dreamworld she had inhabited before the interruption had woken her. She surprised herself with the calm way she was handling things.

Next morning she was up before everybody else and methodically went through the motions of getting herself ready for the short train journey ahead. She was going to take one small bag, and her father had promised to drive up the following weekend for the rest of her things. She knew she would have to

face her parents' gentle inquisition about
Harlem sooner or later, but by now she
regarded that as the lesser of two evils, the
other being the far worse one of fighting it
out with Harlem himself over her decision to
pull the plug on their affair.

Ginny dragged herself out of bed to hug
her goodbye. 'If you change your mind about
anything——' She shrugged. 'Well, you know
where we are.' She accompanied Tiffany as
far as the front door, saying, 'Take care,' as
she made her way down the steps to the road.

At the gate Tiffany turned to wave, then
froze as a taxi drew into the kerb, releasing
a sickeningly familiar figure on to the
pavement.

'Going somewhere, Tiffany?' throbbed the
voice she recognised, as Harlem came up
beside her and tried to take her bag out of
her hand.

'Leave me alone!' With a yelp of dismay
she snatched the bag back again and ran with
it to the top of the steps. Pushing Ginny to
one side, she tried to throw herself back into
the safety of the house and close the door,
but Harlem somehow negotiated the steps
and thrust the full weight of his body against
it so that it flew open again.

'You were here last night, weren't you? This
proves it.' His expression was murderous. As
he heaved his way inside Tiffany dodged past
him, intending to run off down the road and

if need be, hijack the taxi Harlem had just vacated. Then something happened, and instead of safely negotiating the few steps to the bottom, she fell forward with a little scream, landing in a heap with the bag rolling down after her.

Something happened inside her, and everything seemed to swim for a moment. She was aware of Ginny's white face yelling something at Harlem from the top of the steps and his sudden appearance by her side. She felt his arms reach round her and she saw the taxi-driver leave his cab; then she felt herself being carried back inside the house.

There were spasms of pain shooting through her body, and she seemed to hear Harlem's earlier words, when he had told her, 'One small mistake and you might find life changed forever,' and she became aware of anxious faces looking down at her. Then there was a gap when she wasn't sure what was happening, and then an ambulance, the clean white sheets of a hospital bed. And finally oblivion.

When she next opened her eyes Harlem was sitting next to the bed on a wooden hospital chair, his dark, deep eyes drained of energy, staring motionlessly into her face. When he saw she was awake he took her hand. He didn't say anything but simply stroked it, gently, tenderly, as if he felt she might at any moment go away again.

'I feel all right,' she said, struggling to sit up. Then she remembered, and her cheeks flamed as she gave him a quick glance.

'Yes, you're both all right.' His voice was flat, colourless, like his eyes, as lifeless as if he had no energy left.

'Shouldn't you be at the tech. run-through now?' she asked, as brightly as she could.

'Why was I the last to know?' His rhythmic pressure on the back of her hand slowed slightly.

She tried to withdraw it, to turn away, anything but bear the brunt of that dark stare, but he leaned forward and held her face gently in his free hand. 'Why, Tiffany? What did you think I would say?'

'I didn't know how to tell you,' she answered in a small voice, trying to look away. 'You don't want anything permanent. It—it would have looked as if I was trying to hold a gun to your head.'

'You little fool.' He released her and sat looking at the wall on the other side of the bed as if it held some message for him.

'It doesn't matter,' she rushed on. 'I don't want to get married or anything. I've got it all planned. I can keep on working for months yet, and afterwards I should be able to get back to work with no problem. I expect I'll even be able to get some freelance work later—the sort of thing I can do at home.'

'And what about me?'

'What about you?' She gave him a quick glance, but there was nothing in his expression to show what he meant.

He picked up her hand again as if he hadn't seen it before, and studied it carefully. 'Don't I deserve a gun to my head if I walk out on you in these circumstances? Or do you imagine you've managed to get pregnant all by yourself?' His lips lifted slightly. 'Men have rights and responsibilities too, you know.'

'I don't need a husband,' she replied shortly.

'What about our child? Doesn't it need a father?'

'I expect it won't matter much. Why should it? Lots of women are bringing up children by themselves.'

'Not my children.'

She stiffened in the bed. 'I suppose you're going to come on all possessive now. You needn't bother. I know you'd hate to feel tied down. Once you've got used to the novelty of being a father you'll soon lose that possessive feeling.' She avoided his glance. 'Would you mind ringing the bell? I'd like to ask them when I can go home.'

'Where do you intend to go?'

'That's my business.'

'I can order a cab for you, that's all.'

She flinched at the ease with which he accepted her decision. 'It's all right,' she told him, hearing her voice waver. 'I expect one of the nurses will be able to do that.'

He gave a sort of muffled snarl and rose to his feet, pressing the bell as he did so, and when a nurse bobbed her head round the door he was already across the room.

Told that she could leave after lunch, Tiffany eyed Harlem without speaking. 'I'll send a car for you,' he told her curtly. 'If there's nothing wrong with you I want you in the theatre this afternoon. There's a show opening tonight, in case you've forgotten, and you have a contract to fulfil.'

'Harlem!' she called as he opened the door.

'Be there,' he warned

'Wait! Listen—I'm not going back to the way things were. And I've changed my mind about working for you——'

'Obviously. But it takes two to tango, my dear. Or hasn't anybody ever told you that?' He gave her an enigmatic tilt of the lips that sent a swoosh of desire coursing through her despite the way her thoughts were hammering in her head. Then he went out and she was left with the feeling that she had somehow been the loser. She couldn't believe he was so callous as to expect her to work today after what had happened.

'If he seriously expects me to go in this afternoon he's madder than I thought,' she told herself fiercely as she prepared to leave the hospital. When she asked for a taxi she received a surprised look, however. 'There's already someone waiting for you with a car,' she was told.

Full of misgivings, she made her way across the foyer. There was only one exit and she would have to leave that way, but it didn't mean she had to bow to Harlem's will either—there were always taxis bringing visitors up to the doors and she could take one of those. But it wasn't Harlem who waited for her in the visitors' lounge. It was Frank.

He kissed her on the cheek. 'You look fine. How do you feel?'

'One hundred per cent,' she told him. He didn't say anything about her intended absence from the studio and perhaps he didn't know. He simply led her out to his waiting car.

When they reached the theatre he led her into the auditorium to one of the boxes jutting out over the stalls. 'More comfortable here,' he told her as he settled her in one of the red plush armchairs. 'What about having a pot of coffee sent up?'

'Are you going to stay with me, Frank?' she asked as he went to the door at the back of the box.

'Too true. The boys are coming up as well. Curtain up in ten minutes.'

When he'd gone Tiffany peered over the edge of the balustrade. There was quite a crowd down below, more than she would have expected at a dress rehearsal, but then this was a bigger production than usual and was the first full-length show by the new company. Harlem would want as much response as he could get, even though there could be no radical changes at this stage.

There had been no sign of him so far and she didn't expect him to come out front. His time would be amply absorbed by events backstage. Soon Frank returned, Jason and Gavin appeared, and the performance began.

Two hours later there was dead silence from the watchers in the stalls as the lights faded on stage.

'All right, house lights!' It was Harlem's voice calling out of the darkness, and it brought the main lights on, draining the stage instantly of all its magic. It looked workaday under the yellowish light and the dancers themselves seemed garishly dressed, bizarre and over-made-up. Tiffany's breath was held so tightly her ribs began to ache. Harlem himself seemed somehow shrunken too, standing out there as if he was truly alone, the only one not hiding behind a stage mask. He had really put his inmost feelings on the line, revealing his vulnerability, building a show like this. Now her heart went out to him as she understood the courage of what he had done, and she watched him blink against the dazzle of the light with her heart bursting with compassion.

Then she heard something happening down below and, looking over the edge of the balcony into the stalls, she saw to her astonishment the stage crew, front-of-house team and all the other invited guests slowly rising to their feet. One by one they were beginning to applaud. Their individual handclaps sounded strangely thin in the vast dome of the theatre but there was no mistaking the response. They were giving Harlem a standing ovation

Tiffany cast a glance at Frank, but he had risen to his feet too, applauding as if it was a proper performance and not merely a dress rehearsal. Jason leaned forward, gripping her by the shoulder. She saw with astonishment that there were tears streaming down his cheeks. 'That was *so* moving,' he said, giving her shoulder a squeeze. Then he too was rising to his feet shouting, *'Beautiful, beautiful!'* and Gavin joined him, until finally Tiffany was the only one in the whole place who remained seated.

When the noise died down Harlem, still looking small, thanked everyone and rather abruptly told the cast there would be no need for any notes and said he hoped an uneventful dress rehearsal didn't mean a catastrophic first performance. Then, wishing them luck and reminding them what time they were due back, he walked unevenly offstage.

Tiffany felt her senses prickle with alarm. Sure enough, a few minutes later the door at the back of the box opened and he was suddenly there, bulking large and purposefully in the doorway, all illusion of shrunkenness having disappeared. Frank and the others shook him warmly by the hand and slapped him on the back for a few minutes before going out. When she saw them leave she felt like an abandoned ship.

He came to sit on the edge of the balustrade, his long legs stretched out in front of him.

'You changed the ending after all,' she remarked, to break the heavy silence with which he was regarding her. She wondered how she was going to escape.

'I was feeling unexpectedly optimistic at the time,' he told her. 'But there's still time to change it back.'

She looked down at her fingers.

'Tiffany, do you want to talk here or go somewhere else——?' he began.

'I don't want to talk anywhere,' she told him. 'I don't think there's anything to be said. I know how you feel. You know how I feel. End of story.'

'I'm not sure you do know how I feel.' He paused. 'And you still haven't answered the question I asked you this morning.'

'What question?' she asked stubbornly, feeling she could guess which one.

'I asked you why I was the last to know. Frank knew.'

'He guessed. He's a clever, sensitive man——'

'Of course he is. He's one of my best friends.'

'Don't make claims for yourself on that basis,' she broke in.

He gave a wry smile. 'As if I would. Still,' he shrugged, 'your friend Ginny knew and for all I know half of London did, too.' He looked puzzled. 'But the one person who should have known didn't.' He paused. 'Was I supposed to have been able to work it out? If so, I certainly failed. Was that it? Was I supposed to guess?'

'What difference would it have made?' she asked.

'None,' he agreed. 'If you really do want to go ahead and become a single mother that's your privilege. But I don't intend to give up *all* my rights, whatever you seem to feel about my suitability as a father.'

'I can't stop you taking a hand, I suppose, if you insist,' she grudgingly admitted. 'Though I'd rather we just made it a clean break.'

'I'd rather we didn't make it a break at all,' he said swiftly. 'When I came back after the summer I wasn't sure what the hell I felt about anything. I felt I had to give us both space and time. Then I'm afraid my resolution failed and I—well, I couldn't resist taking you to bed again and, as I thought, keeping some control over the situation . . .'

'Yes, I was a private version of your dancers,' she said bitterly. 'Wind me up and wind me down—and kick me out when you get bored in a week or two.'

'I won't get bored with you in a week or in a year,' he told her. 'It'll take this lifetime and the next at least. And what's this about kicking you out?'

'That's what you implied yesterday afternoon, remember? Move in for a couple of weeks, you said!'

He sighed. 'I thought about what I'd asked you during the rest of the afternoon, and I realised I hadn't put it quite the way I meant to. If you'd given me the chance last night I had been going to put it another way.'

'Which way?' she asked suspiciously.

His eyes raked her face. 'I was going to ask you to marry me.'

'You were?' She felt herself go very still, but her eyes were wide with disbelief.

He shrugged. 'It was a crazy idea that struck me in the middle of rehearsals. It was like Newton's apple,' he explained. 'Or a light bulb exploding above my head. I couldn't see why I hadn't thought of it before. Except perhaps that I probably thought you wouldn't be keen on the idea . . .'

'And you're not the marrying type.' Tiffany glared across at him. 'So what now?'

'Well . . .' He looked down at her. 'You're obviously hell-bent on becoming a single mother, so I guess I'll have to think again.' His voice dropped an interval and he leaned forward. 'Unless there's a hint of a chance I can persuade you to change your mind?'

'How do I know you're not just inventing this whole story because you have an exaggerated sense of duty?' she asked in a small voice.

'Treating you like a kind of charity act, you mean?' He regarded her with a slight smile curving his lips.

She nodded. 'I'm not marrying anybody under conditions like that. If I weren't going to have a baby the thought of marrying me would never have crossed your mind.' She looked away.

'You can check that with Frank,' he told her quietly.

'What on earth's Frank got to do with it?'

'Well . . .' He shifted his legs for a moment. 'After my brilliant idea in rehearsal yesterday—before I discovered you were pregnant, note—I wanted to do something about it straight away. But you'd disappeared and I bumped into Frank as he was leaving. Not being entirely sure what the situation between you two had been while I was away, I thought it only fair to mention I thought it was time I got around to asking you to marry me. He was all for it. Ask him yourself. I also learned,' he added in a kind of aside, 'my return hadn't upset anything that might have been going on in the summer . . .'

'How considerate!' She wasn't sure she liked being discussed in this way behind her back.

'I thought it was considerate too.' He reached out and took her hands in his. 'After that I came looking for you. The elusive Miss Mulgrove,' he admonished. 'You really have led me a dance, one way and another.' He looked serious for a minute. 'Though I must admit without your remark about love being a sort of redemption I might not have seen sense even now.'

'I'm glad I've done something right,' she remarked, trying not to show how wild his touch was making her feel. He was holding both her hands, his thumbs moving rhythmically back and forth over the insides of her wrists. Her knees felt trembly, and she was glad she was still sitting down.

'The first time I saw you I admit I was wary of you,' he explained. 'I guessed you would get through to me and undermine my control if I let you. At first I thought it was simply your sense of chaos that would upset things—the power of those hazy violet eyes of yours . . Later I realised it went deeper than that.'

She allowed him to pull her up so that despite her shaky knees she was standing against him, looking up. 'It was horrible when we bumped into each other after you'd been away. Frank told me you needed to come to terms with the car smash, and all the time you were away I tried to tell myself to be patient—that you *would* come back to me, given time. But when we met—' her voice shook at the memory '—we were like strangers . . . and when we started to work together you seemed like a man living on another planet—you were very physical,' her mind flew to the nights when he had taken her to his bed, his hands running sensually over her body as if he could never touch her enough, just as they were beginning to now— 'but your mind seemed to be elsewhere . . .'

She tried to concentrate, giving him a little frown, but her eyes softened as they travelled over the planes and hollows of his face and she saw the harsh lines of exhaustion beginning to relax.

'I couldn't understand what you wanted,' she murmured, leaning against him and giving up all thoughts of resisting. 'You seemed to think your feelings would burn themselves out—and you were switched off completely during the day . . . Maybe it was because you were working on the new show, but it was confusing—it made me think you really didn't care, even when at night you really seemed to! And I couldn't stand it when you kept trying to pretend nothing was happening between us—especially when your kisses exploded fireworks for me. You were so cool, in control. The dance master and his clockwork toys.'

'That was when I was struggling to make sense of it by trying to keep you at a distance.' He looked suitably contrite. 'I was scared to admit I couldn't control what I felt. At night was the only time I dared risk it. Then I began to find I couldn't do without you during the day, either. In fact, what I really wanted was to surrender to you completely, but I couldn't let myself. I was afraid of losing it all . . . I dared not trust life again . . . I felt if I loved you too much you'd be snatched away from me . . .' A shadow briefly passed over his face as a memory of the crash returned. He glanced down at his stick, and tapped his leg with it. 'I had doubts about asking you to face life with this, too.'

'You're more vigorous now than most men ever have been or ever will be!' Impatient to feel his lips on hers, she reached up and pulled his head down.

But he held back a moment longer. 'When you vanished yesterday,' he told her, his voice thickening, 'It was the end of all my doubts. I knew there was no other answer.' He lifted her chin. 'Say yes, Tiffany? Will you marry me?'

'Harlem . . . do you think I can live without you? I need you night and day . . . I love you so very much. A long time ago you told me I needed to come out of my cosy shell, and since meeting you and feeling I was going to lose you I've walked through fire. But it's made me grow up. I'm a woman now, not a girl, and I know I'm ready to marry you and love and,' she glanced down, 'care for our baby too.'

'If I hurt you, Tiffany, I'm sorry . . .' He held her tightly. 'I just thought you'd be happier in the long run with someone else. Frank, for instance——'

'Harlem!' She stood on tiptoe and planted a small kiss on his lips. 'It's you I'm crazy for. Ever since I saw you looking at me in such amazement when I threw myself at your feet I've known you were going to mean something very special in my life.' She added softly, 'Don't you see, I'm at your feet now just as I was then.'

'No.' He began to kiss her without holding back. 'I want you right beside me, Tiffany. Always and forever . . . Sharing control, giving it and taking it . . . Only you, my love—and,' he raised his head for a moment and his hand skimmed her still shapely figure, 'this little dancing love-child of ours.'

PASSPORT TO ROMANCE VACATION SWEEPSTAKES

OFFICIAL RULES

SWEEPSTAKES RULES AND REGULATIONS. NO PURCHASE NECESSARY.

HOW TO ENTER:

1. To enter, complete this official entry form and return with your invoice in the envelope provided, or print your name, address, telephone number and age on a plain piece of paper and mail to: Passport to Romance, P.O. Box #1397, Buffalo, N.Y. 14269-1397 No mechanically reproduced entries accepted.
2. All entries must be received by the Contest Closing Date, midnight, December 31, 1990 to be eligible.
3. Prizes: There will be ten (10) Grand Prizes awarded, each consisting of a choice of a trip for two people to: i) London, England (approximate retail value $5,050 U.S.); ii) England, Wales and Scotland (approximate retail value $6,400 U.S.); iii) Caribbean Cruise (approximate retail value $7,300 U.S.); iv) Hawaii (approximate retail value $ 9,550 U.S.); v) Greek Island Cruise in the Mediterranean (approximate retail value $12,250 U.S.); vi) France (approximate retail value $7,300 U.S.).
4. Any winner may choose to receive any trip or a cash alternative prize of $5,000.00 U.S. in lieu of the trip.
5. Odds of winning depend on number of entries received.
6. A random draw will be made by Nielsen Promotion Services, an independent judging organization on January 29, 1991, in Buffalo, N.Y., at 11:30 a.m. from all eligible entries received on or before the Contest Closing Date. Any Canadian entrants who are selected must correctly answer a time-limited, mathematical skill-testing question in order to win. Quebec residents may submit any litigation respecting the conduct and awarding of a prize in this contest to the Régie des loteries et courses du Quebec.
7. Full contest rules may be obtained by sending a stamped, self-addressed envelope to: "Passport to Romance Rules Request", P.O. Box 9998, Saint John, New Brunswick, E2L 4N4.
8. Payment of taxes other than air and hotel taxes is the sole responsibility of the winner.
9. Void where prohibited by law.

PASSPORT TO ROMANCE VACATION SWEEPSTAKES

OFFICIAL RULES

SWEEPSTAKES RULES AND REGULATIONS. NO PURCHASE NECESSARY.

HOW TO ENTER:

1. To enter, complete this official entry form and return with your invoice in the envelope provided, or print your name, address, telephone number and age on a plain piece of paper and mail to: Passport to Romance, P.O. Box #1397, Buffalo, N.Y. 14269-1397 No mechanically reproduced entries accepted.
2. All entries must be received by the Contest Closing Date, midnight, December 31, 1990 to be eligible.
3. Prizes: There will be ten (10) Grand Prizes awarded, each consisting of a choice of a trip for two people to: i) London, England (approximate retail value $5,050 U.S.); ii) England, Wales and Scotland (approximate retail value $6,400 U.S.); iii) Caribbean Cruise (approximate retail value $7,300 U.S.); iv) Hawaii (approximate retail value $ 9,550 U.S.); v) Greek Island Cruise in the Mediterranean (approximate retail value $12,250 U.S.); vi) France (approximate retail value $7,300 U.S.).
4. Any winner may choose to receive any trip or a cash alternative prize of $5,000.00 U.S. in lieu of the trip.
5. Odds of winning depend on number of entries received.
6. A random draw will be made by Nielsen Promotion Services, an independent judging organization on January 29, 1991, in Buffalo, N.Y., at 11:30 a.m. from all eligible entries received on or before the Contest Closing Date. Any Canadian entrants who are selected must correctly answer a time-limited, mathematical skill-testing question in order to win. Quebec residents may submit any litigation respecting the conduct and awarding of a prize in this contest to the Régie des loteries et courses du Quebec.
7. Full contest rules may be obtained by sending a stamped, self-addressed envelope to: "Passport to Romance Rules Request", P.O. Box 9998, Saint John, New Brunswick, E2L 4N4.
8. Payment of taxes other than air and hotel taxes is the sole responsibility of the winner.
9. Void where prohibited by law.

RLS-DIR

VACATION SWEEPSTAKES

Official Entry Form

Yes, enter me in the drawing for one of ten Vacations-for-Two! If I'm a winner, I'll get my choice of any of the six different destinations being offered — and I won't have to decide until after I'm notified!

Return entries with invoice in envelope provided along with Daily Travel Allowance Voucher. Each book in your shipment has two entry forms — and the more you enter, the better your chance of winning!

Name _____

Address _____ Apt. _____

City _____ State/Prov. _____ Zip/Postal Code _____

Daytime phone number _____
Area Code

☐ I am enclosing a Daily Travel
Allowance Voucher in the amount of $ _____ Write in amount
revealed beneath scratch-off

© 1990 HARLEQUIN ENTERPRISES LTD.

PASSPORT
WIN
1 of 10 Vacations
SEE INSIDE
TO ROMANCE

MONTH 2
ENTRY

VACATION SWEEPSTAKES

Official Entry Form

Yes, enter me in the drawing for one of ten Vacations-for-Two! If I'm a winner, I'll get my choice of any of the six different destinations being offered — and I won't have to decide until after I'm notified!

Return entries with invoice in envelope provided along with Daily Travel Allowance Voucher. Each book in your shipment has two entry forms — and the more you enter, the better your chance of winning!

Name _____

Address _____ Apt. _____

City _____ State/Prov. _____ Zip/Postal Code _____

Daytime phone number _____
Area Code

☐ I am enclosing a Daily Travel
Allowance Voucher in the amount of $ _____ Write in amount
revealed beneath scratch-off

CPS-TWO